MYSTERY MEN

(& WOMEN)

Volume One

I0619511

Airship 27 Productions

Mystery Men (& Women)
Volume One

Updated collection ©2022 Airship 27 Productions

An Airship 27 Production
www.airship27.com

Editor: Ron Fortier
Associate Editor: Charles Saunders
Production Designer: Rob Davis.

ISBN: 978-1-953589-21-7

Printed in the United States of America

10 9 8 7 6 5 4 3 2 1

MYSTERY MEN (& Women)

–Table of Contents–

The Bagman:

The Badge of the Butcher
by B. C. Bell

Chapter I
Chicago 1933

Frank "Mac" McCullough hadn't even finished unpacking the morning deliveries when he heard something so stupid his head almost exploded. Mac's Tobacco had only been open a week, and it was evident that he needed to hire some help. Mac had been working while politely half-listening to one of the customers. He'd only just torn the string from a bundle of new magazines when he heard the words:

"— 'cause ya know, mister, accidents can happen." And then the man had knocked a rack of candy off the counter, which—as noted in the Dictionary of Racketeering—is translatable to only one word: Protection.

The cigar store owner's face snapped into a blank unbelieving stare. His body froze as if he couldn't control his muscle movements and comprehend the depth of the man's idiocy at the same time. The cover of the latest Detective Fiction Weekly remained pinched between Mac's index finger and thumb, as the rest of the magazine tore itself away from the cover, in agonizingly slow motion, and dropped to the floor.

Only a couple of weeks ago Mac, posing as The Bagman, had disposed of neighborhood crime boss, Slots Lurie, and already the local goon factory was fighting over the scraps. Or, as the case may be, the local vultures were just trying to con an extra buck into the till before the next kingpin arrived.

"What's your name, kid?" Mac asked.

"Strother. Strother Cornbluth"

Weird kid, weird name, Mac thought. "Who do you work for?"

The local protection rep stammered. He'd had his speech all rehearsed and hadn't left himself any spaces for questions. Mac didn't know what the guy had been expecting to deal with, but evidently he was counting on the local merchants to roll over like a bunch of sheep herders in a Western B-movie. If Mr. Protection Racket had been expecting cowardly shopkeepers—he was in the wrong town. Poor little guy would've been killed and eaten by the time he'd made corner saloon.

"I said, 'Who do you work for?'" Mac repeated slowly, as if the racketeer had a hearing problem.

"Mister Lloyd Everett," the gangster replied, holding his head high like Mac should be impressed.

"Stinky?" Mac said. "You work for Stinky Everett?" Mac circled the counter about the same time as the puzzled look came across the gangster's face. "Mister, I've known Stinky since he was stealing paste from the nuns in second grade—and nobody called him Lloyd back then. You tell him before any cash passes hands, Mac

McCullough wants to talk to him face to face."

Then he grabbed the man by the back of the pants and collar, and proceeded to give him the bum's rush to the door. The would-be gangster managed to keep his feet moving as fast as the rest of his body for two long shaky strides before his knees buckled and he collapsed outside on the curb. When he got back up and dusted himself off, Mac was already looking down the street ignoring him.

The would-be-gangster tried to stare down a passing junk vendor, but it was evident the immigrant on the wagon was a lot tougher than he was. The gangster-wannabe scratched his head, straightened his hat, and pulled the bill down just low enough to claim whatever happened—it hadn't been him. He sulked off down the alley across the street. Mac continued to eye a Buick Club sedan parked at the next intersection.

The car was parked in front of the First State Bank of Chicago, just down the block, where Lincoln and Marshfield formed a three-way intersection. Exhaust fumes wafted from the tailpipe, distorting the view in waves of summer heat. The driver sat behind the wheel, glancing back and forth, then anxiously back at his watch. Mac had seen a few wheelmen in his time, and all of them had looked pretty much like this guy parked in front of the bank.

Mac stepped back into the store.

When he came back out, he had a Colt Snubnose in the shoulder holster beneath his summer sport coat, and a felt hat wedged on his head. He hung the "back in five minutes" sign on the door, gave the wooden Indian a pat on the head, and then shuffled down the block with his hands in his pockets. One held a mask, the other a handful of braided twine from the cigar store's morning deliveries.

About halfway down the block Mac's brisk stride began to slow down a little. He was still gleaning what was going on, and had little-to-no idea what he was about to do.

So far the entire bank job was text book. The getaway driver sat just behind the bank entrance with the engine running, so he could pull out easily and be moving even as the robbers climbed into the vehicle. Mac could already sense a presence just inside the bank's door. That would be the lookout. He'd be holding a shotgun. One other man would take inside by the counters; that guy would be holding a Thompson Submachine gun on the crowd, keeping everybody calm and in order, choosing the hostages if need be. That left at least one more guy to work inside the counter and get to the safe. A minimum of three armed men inside the bank.

He couldn't figure out a safe way to stop these goons. They were probably armed to the teeth—and, if anything went wrong; people were going to get hurt. Before he got to the corner, he stopped, pretended to look at his watch, and turned into the mouth of the alley across the street from where Stinky Junior had run. For a moment Mac considered firing his gun into the air a few times to alert the cops, but decided they'd only bring more stray bullets.

McCullough hated banks as much as the next guy, probably more—which wasn't necessarily an easy thing to do during The Depression—but thanks to his "extra-legal" background he'd never required the services of a bank for anything other than cashing a check until recently. But at the same time, this crime was a local job. This particular bank was in his neighborhood, where people he knew—mostly-good-people—kept their mostly-hard-earned cash. Never mind that Mac had twenty-grand in stolen mob money stuffed in one of the safe deposit boxes.

He reminded himself the government had yet to declare any federal bank insurance coverage. And, knowing this neighborhood, the stupid bankers probably weren't even covered. But it was ultimately the safety deposit box that made McCullough turn around. As far as Mac was concerned that was public money, money for The Bagman's war on crime. And some minor expenses.

He pulled the mask out of his pocket. He'd only had it a couple of weeks. It was made out of chamois cloth and fit over his head like a tube, covering his entire face except for the eyes. Before that he'd covered his head with a paper bag. The newspapers had called him The Bagman—irony being that he'd been a bagman for the mob at the time. It was a very private joke.

He pulled the mask over his head, tugging at the laces on the sides to tighten it, and then wedged his hat on low with the brim snapped. He pulled his sport coat's lapels up and strolled down the sidewalk, toward the bank, as if he were looking at his shoes, watching his step; anything but hiding his face and stopping a bank robbery.

The bank's location was not textbook for a robbery. First State of Chicago sat in-between—instead of directly on the corner of—two major intersections. Then again, the job itself might be pulled off without being noticed.

The getaway was the problem. The bank sat at a T-shaped intersection, on top of the "T," where the two streets met. To get away, the gang would have to pass the one-way street in front of them that dead ended in front of the bank. They'd have to drive a block to School Street. Then they'd be forced turn left and toward the lake, because School was a one-way street, too. Apparently, they were counting on the element of surprise.

Mac looked up out of his coat only once as he approached the getaway car from the rear, skulking behind sidewalk displays and storefront entrances for cover.

The wheelman was so busy glancing back and forth from the rear view mirror, to the bank and back at his watch, that he never even saw The Bagman coming. A chamois-cloth glove looped the braided twine around the wheelman's neck from behind, like a garrote, and yanked hard enough on both ends to get drivers attention. You could see the wheelman's head rise the harder Mac pulled. It reminded him of one of those acrobatic push-puppets, where you press on the base and Popeye or Krazy Kat spin around the trapeze.

The driver gagged like he was going to throw up. Then a compressed sound, like a Bronx cheer gone wrong rasped out of his throat. His first thought was that the man had no face. Then, glancing in the rear-view, he realized the stranger was wearing a mask—and strangling him. His hands flew to his throat but the cords were already too tight. He reached for his gun, but the man with no face beat him to it, snatching the automatic from under the driver's coat. Arms flailing, unable to breathe, the driver decided to call the job off, honk the horn. Something hit him between the eyes.

The wheelman was so busy glancing back and forth from the rear view mirror, to the bank and back at his watch, that he never even saw The Bagman coming.

Mac let go of the twine, shaking his right hand in the air to get the circulation going again. He hadn't hit the guy, just cut off his air supply and watched him thrash around a little while. Same result.

The Bagman stuck the automatic in his belt, and sat the driver upright again, with his hands dangling limply inside the wheel. The man was unconscious, not dead; it looked like he was sleeping—which Mac thought would be pretty funny when the rest of the gang hopped in the car.

He may not have had a plan, but he had a sense of humor.

A small group of people gathered catty-corner from the getaway car. Somebody yelled, "You! In the street! What are you doing? Is everything all right?"

The Bagman finished propping up the unconscious body's head and turned toward the crowd. When an older woman saw his mask, he could see her flinch. A man pointed at him. Mac couldn't hear what the guy said, but he looked excited.

"Hey buddy! Could you do me a favor?" The Bagman tried to yell and whisper at the same time, as if that would keep the people calm.

The older woman screamed and pulled a hatpin out of her pancake panama. Wielding it like a knife, she sprinted to the middle of the block—toward a police emergency callbox. Mac groaned under his breath and strode gently toward the small group on the corner. The gawkers huddled into a bunch and shuffled off as one—backwards, still staring at him—and toward the old lady on the call box. All of them except for a tall, young man in a straw hat.

"Hey, bud. Seriously, I'm trying to make sure nobody gets hurt, that's all." The Bagman reached into his hip pocket, and the boyish-man flinched.

When Mac's hand came out holding a ten dollar bill, one of the young man's eyebrows disappeared with interest beneath the flat brim of his hat.

"All you got to do is get down to that callbox while the old broad there is still on it. Tell 'em there's a grease fire—" Mac glanced past Marshfield Avenue and guessed at an address, "—Tell 'em there's a grease fire in back of 1622 School Street! It's out of control in the back kitchen, and they're going to have to pull up in the yard! You got that?"

"Sure."

"There's another ten in it for you if they get here in time."

The young man held his hand out.

"IF they get here in time. You can pick it up from one of the clerks in that cigar store." Mac pointed at his shop, then jogged back over to the getaway car.

By now, the lookout inside the bank door had to have known something was going on. If Mac just barged in the door he'd be pouring buckshot out of his mask for a week. With no time, and no plan, he simply stopped—just standing there, halfway out in the street, staring at the unconscious wheelman and rubbing his leather-faced jaw with the inside of his hand. When he looked down the street, he realized he was a target. The gang might not be able to see him this second, but as soon as they left the building they'd be shooting Bagmen in a barrel.

Any other man in this situation would have been sweating. Here he was, a masked, wanted man, standing near the middle of an intersection in broad daylight, about to face down a gang of bank robbers. People in the street were calling the cops. Bullets were about to fly. Most men would have frozen in panic, or run away. The Bagman just kept staring at the getaway car with his chin cupped in his fist. Then his eyes widened, and he inhaled deeply.

He was thinking about Babe Ruth.

"Show me a typical American boy and I'll show you a boy with a pocket knife in one hand and a baseball bat in the other. Now you can get a knife in the shape of a baseball bat and I'm mighty glad it carries my signature. It's a good knife and a good idea. Yours truly, Babe Ruth" Mac had seen the sign at Woolworth's about two years ago. When his hand came out of his pocket, he was already flicking the blade out.

It was a good knife.

He took one last glance at the Babe's autograph on the handle and cut the valve stems off the tires on the street side of the car, where the gangsters couldn't see. Then he jabbed the knife into the rear tire next to the sidewalk, yanking the blade out as he walked, rather than slashing the tire. He'd been afraid of breaking the Babe's blade; and this way it would be a slow leak. Maybe the bank robbers wouldn't notice.

Then, the Bagman ambled toward the north side of the bank, ducked around the corner, and ran away.

"We got hostages in here, and we ain't afraid of shooting 'em!" Somebody with a voice like torn metal yelled from the swaying bank door. After a long silence, a head appeared, looking both ways. "OK! We're coming out!" the voice yelled as if he were actually talking to someone. "But if anything funny happens—we got hostages!" Machinegun fire blasted out the window. Bullets chopped holes in a dotted line down the street. There was another burst of gunfire. One of the gangsters screamed unintelligible orders, and another one ran out the door.

The first man exited waving a Thompson Submachine gun and firing into the air. He spun around to make sure no one was hiding in front of the bank, then stationed himself outside to cover the others.

A frail-looking man in a blue pinstripe suit stepped out of the bank after him. He had a woman in a headlock, the barrel of an automatic pressed to her temple. The next goon out carried a sawed off shotgun. He made for the passenger's front seat, standing just outside the door, waving for the lookout with the machinegun to follow.

As the machine gunner made for his seat, the frail man pushed his hostage into the rear and climbed into the car next to her. Settled comfortably in the back seat, he told the unconscious driver to "get the lead out." The only response was a siren in the distance. He screamed at the driver. The sirens just got louder. Everybody in the car began yelling at each other until; finally, the frail man got out and dumped the driver in the street.

The frail man's mouth flew open with a string of curses as the driver's head bounced off the pavement. And when he looked back up his hostage had already jumped out of the back of the car and sprinted across the street. Sirens echoed from everywhere.

The frail man formed some not so fragile words, jumped behind the wheel and cranked the starter. Gears grinded and the car spun out into the avenue headed south, not quite rolling on its rims. At the same time two radio squad cars peeled toward the corner a block behind them, closing in fast.

The Buick hopped across the Marshfield intersection without even braking. A Model-A bounced across Lincoln Avenue and into a driveway ahead of them, every other car remained stopped. The frail man punched the gas. What was left of the tires squealed, and the sedan picked up speed, pulling around the Model-A, almost forcing it off the road. If the Buick could make the next intersection and turn left before the police saw them, they might just get away clean.

The entire getaway car leaned to the right as the frail man yanked the wheel left. The two squad cars rounded the curve just in time to see…nothing. There was a Model-A double parked, but the driver was already moving out of the way. The police car slowed in front of the bank to investigate. The old man behind the wheel of the Ford started waving his arm out of the side of the car, pointing and hollering. The police, unable to turn left on Marshfield, sped on to one-way School Street and hung a hard left.

The police car's driver was forced to hit the brakes and went into a skid.

A fire truck was blocking the right lane and most of the street. The bank robbers were still waving their guns around and yelling orders at traffic when the police car hit them from behind. The officers in the first car stepped out. One had a Submachine gun, the other a shotgun. So did the cops in the car behind them.

A big man in shirtsleeves stepped out from behind a newsstand, his copper hair blowing in the summer breeze, and applauded. Then he headed back to the cigar store.

Chapter 2
The Hellfighter

At the corner of Lincoln and Addison, hidden in the shadows behind a hot dog stand under the Ravenswood El, sat the best auto repair garage in Chicago. Of course, nobody would have noticed the place if it wasn't for a sign that read "Crankshaft's Car Repair & Sales" in immaculate antique lettering. And, nobody would have noticed that sign, if it hadn't been for another two-foot sign above it portraying the silhouette of a doughboy from The Great War, charging over a ribbon that read "369th Infantry Division."

The 369th, better known as The Harlem Hellfighters, was the hardest fighting division on the Western Front. The German's had originally thought the black soldiers would be pushovers. They weren't, and the Krauts wound up naming them the Hellfighters. Antoine "Crankshaft" Jones had been a hero overseas, and awarded the French equivalent of the Medal of Honor, the Croix De Guerre. He was also

Mac's oldest friend, and a begrudging partner of The Bagman.

The front gate was already barred by a brand new padlock, but Mac could tell from the light inside Crankshaft's office that the ace mechanic was still there. He picked the lock and let himself in, steering around the piles of used parts, scraps, and junked cars that had been scavenged to rebuild the others.

As soon as he reached the tin shack that operated as both office and garage, Mac let himself in. Crankshaft sat behind his desk with a .45 Automatic aimed at Mac's face. He put the gun down when he saw who it was, and without saying a word, pulled a bottle out of the desk drawer, filling two small cups with bootleg moonshine.

"No alcohol yet, Crank. Got some business to take care of tonight and I was wondering if you might want to tag along, take the Blue Streak out for a run."

The Graham-Paige "Blue Streak," a sports car Mac had stolen from the mob, had been state of the art before Crankshaft had gotten his hands on it. Since then, its state had been pushed even farther, and the brand new eight-cylinder had become The Bagman's choice for burning the midnight oil. With a new suspension system, and wider tires Crank's souped-up Blue Streak could outmaneuver anything on the road.

"It should be a milk run, but who knows," Mac finished.

Crankshaft poured the whiskey back into its battle-scarred bottle, and put it back in the desk. He muttered, "Waste not, want not," under his breath, but Mac knew Crank was the kind of guy that never wanted prohibition to end, because he actually liked the bootleg sour mash.

Discretion being the better part of valor, Mac neglected to mention that little observation, and sat backwards in the chair across from Crankshaft's desk. The ace mechanic stood over the slop sink, scrubbing the oil from his hands as Mac went over the details of his day.

"So you're not worried about somebody identifying the store clerk who came out and applauded the arrest?" Crankshaft said.

"Nah, nobody even noticed me. And besides, it was kind of neat the way the cops boxed 'em in. Gangsters couldn't even turn around without dropping their guns first."

"So now you're going to give your old buddy in the protection racket a visit as The Bagman? Let him know who supposedly runs the neighborhood?"

"Supposedly, yes—only without the 'supposedly,'" Mac said. "Problem with this whole crime-fighting thing is that when you stop one crook, there's always somebody there to fill in for him. I stopped one racket, and now every lowlife in town is fighting over the scraps."

"Way things are going you're going to need a mob of your own."

"What I could really use is a decent clerk for the store," Mac said. "I haven't had any free time in a week, and as much as I enjoy cigars and magazines, I'd forgotten something…"

"What's that?"

"I enjoy them alone. I got nothing against people—you know that, Crank—it's just that…well, some of 'em are just boring. I never noticed before how everybody tells the guy behind the counter their entire philosophy, but it never seems to have anything to do with listening. Do you know how many times this week I've had to say 'This is a cigar store not a library!'? to scare loafers away from the magazine racks? I lost count."

"So now what? You want to sell the store you just opened?"

"Nah, not really. Just have to re-map the course of my empire." Mac winked when he said it. "I was thinking more along the lines of using it as a front. That way I'd still get the fringe benefits, and occasionally even enjoy going inside."

"So why don't you just hire some of your friends to run it?"

"Because most of my friends are crooks, and I don't think I could trust the ones that aren't."

"Too honest, huh?"

"No, not too honest. I just don't want 'em getting hurt by what they don't know."

"Or what they might find out?"

"That too. Nah, my best bet is to either find somebody I know that's looking for honest work, and threaten their life if anything ever comes up missing—or find someone that's just a little between."

"Between?"

"Good and evil."

"Forget it. Threaten your friends."

With that, Crankshaft snapped a pair of reflective goggles on over his drivers cap, and locked the office door, which seemed more like ceremony than security to Mac since the place was about to fall down. Then the two men walked behind a scrap pile and disappeared in the darkness. Less than a minute later, two headlights rose out of hell, swerved around the scattered wreckage, and cut through the night headed west.

❀ ❀ ❀

The suburb of Niles Center had a lot in common with Stinky Everett. Not only were they both outside The Loop, so to speak, but the two of them had both been campaigning to switch back to their original names for years. The citizens of Niles Center wanted to go back to their Indian name, Skokie, so they wouldn't be confused with the nearby town of Niles. Stinky just didn't want to be called Stinky anymore.

After a decade of grief because the name "Stinky" had stuck, Everett moved out of the city in an effort to escape his moniker. He'd been lucky enough to move into one of the neighborhood's abandoned bungalows when the Crash of '29 had stopped all construction in town. Since then, he had been dabbling in mail fraud out of a house on Dempster Street.

Not only was his hygiene bad, but so was his choice of crimes, Mac thought. Smart guys didn't commit federal crimes; they paid other people to commit them. Pretty soon the FBI was going to be carrying guns, and the idea of getting shot for a dollar an envelope seemed about as reasonable as bobbing for piranha. Maybe that's why the Stinkster was thinking about the protection rackets.

Luckily, Mac had heard about Stinky's operation a while back and knew where Everett's house was. He was counting on him not being smart enough to have relocated.

When the Blue Streak drifted up behind the house on Dempster, the only light on inside shone from a ground level window. Mac told Crankshaft to stay in the car. Crankshaft ignored him, stepped to the back of the roadster and pulled a Thompson Submachine gun from under the rumble seat.

"C'mon, Crank, just stay in the car. We may have to make a getaway," Mac whispered, as he slid toward the back door.

"Getaways are for crooks and mobsters. In case you haven't noticed, I'm neither."

"Yeah, well in case you haven't noticed, I'm supposed to be some kind of outlaw, and the mob wants me dead."

"Who doesn't. Now open the damn door, you know this is a two man job."

Mac pulled the lockpick set out of his pocket and gently inserted two of its stems into a top of the line Schlade bolt lock embedded in the door. It took ten seconds to put one of the picks on top and the tension wrench along the bottom of the keyhole. Mac's shoulder twitched once, the lock made a ratcheting sound, and the bolt clicked open. The masked man held the doorknob with one hand pulling, as the other pressed against the door. A thin shaft of light pierced through the fraction of an opening. A radio played swing jazz in the background. Count Basie?

Mac took his hat off, put it on the tip of his fingers and stuck it into the sliver of light, waiting for somebody to shoot him in the hand. Nobody did. He waved Crankshaft over to the right side of the door, gently nudged it open, and put his back to the wall on the left. Nothing but "Stormy Weather" playing in the background.

And the smell of death.

The Bagman slid through the back door, signaling Crankshaft to be quiet. He was reaching for a handkerchief to cover his nose when he saw the body. Lloyd "Stinky" Everett was face down, sitting at a workbench, surrounded by stacks of envelopes and mail order pamphlets. Mac picked up one entitled "How to Escape a Bank Vault," and pushed Everett's hair around. There was a hole in the back of his head, probably never knew what hit him.

"Notice anything funny?" he whispered.

"Not enough blood. Probably dead when they shot him," Crankshaft whispered. "Check out upstairs?"

Mac nodded.

Or rather, The Bagman nodded, Crank thought. The normally impish eyes behind the mask had gone cold. Crankshaft had seen men in the trenches with that look during the war.

The Man With No Face pushed things around on the table with the mail order pamphlet, stopped, and held up Stinky's open palm. It was burned, blistered. Not blistered by fire; there was some sort of brown residue in a straight line. The masked man looked up, turned his head searching the room, then walked over to a tin bucket in the corner. Tapping it with his toe, water sloshed over its edge.

Crankshaft didn't bother to ask why the Bagman pushed one of the man's pant legs up to his knee. But the man's leg had more blood on it than his head.

Entering the kitchen door, The Bagman simply kicked it in and dived. Spinning in the air, he landed on his back while sliding under the kitchen table, his Colt Snubnose aimed at the rest of the room.

"Yoo-hoo! Fuller Brush Man!" he yelled. "We really do have a brush for every cleaning need!" Count Basie turned into a commercial for Blue Coal; so it was the radio and not a record player. "Check the closets, I'll look under the bed," Mac said, getting up.

Crankshaft went to the entry hall. He opened the closet door, moving as if he were a part of it—so his back was to the wall when the gun in the closet went off.

Shreds of cloth popped into the entry hall like feathers out of a pillow. Plaster jumped from the bullet hole in the wall and met them in midair.

The ace mechanic kicked the door closed, and strafed the floor in front of it with machinegun fire. He pulled his reflective goggles back down to hide his face, and yelled:

"Drop the gun and step out with your hands in the air..." The WLS Barn Dance emanated from the radio in the background. Crank hated Hillbilly music. "Stupid's only going to get you shot nine ways to Sunday," he finished.

A silver-plated .45 automatic clattered on the floor, and two hands extended from inside the closet. A young man's profile stepped into the scattered light from the window.

"Aw Jeez—" Mac moaned, over Crankshafts shoulder.

Crankshaft jumped, surprised. He hadn't known Mac was behind him. He did manage to pull the instinctive blow of the Tommygun butt to Mac's stomach—but he still hit him hard enough to teach him a lesson.

"—It's the budding young racketeer," Mac wheezed, pointing, and clutching his belly.

"The kid from the—?"

"Future Felons of America," Mac interrupted. He didn't want to mention the cigar store. "What's the story, morning glory?"

"B-Buh-Buh..." the young man stammered.

"It's the Barn Dance, kid—" Mac thumbed over his shoulder at the radio "—not Bing Crosby."

"Bagman!" he bleated.

"Yes. And what should I call you, Killer?"

The kid opened his mouth and Crankshaft hit him in the side of the head with the Tommygun butt. Mac looked on open mouthed as the body fell to the floor.

"Damn, Crank! You nuts? I'm trying to question the little gink."

"Question him somewhere else. Case you hadn't noticed, I just fired a Tommy gun in the city limits."

"Well, that would explain the sirens in the fiddle music—but I wouldn't exactly call this a city—"

"You enjoy getting on my nerves, don't you?" Crankshaft grabbed the kid under one arm and started to drag him.

Mac grabbed him under the other, smiling beneath the mask.

They had to pull a cache of guns and ammo out of the rumble seat and put it up front before they could lay the kid down, his feet hanging over the right side of the car. The Blue Streak's engine purred and its colors merged with the night.

"Where do you want to take him?" Crankshaft asked, turning the car back toward the city, sticking to the back streets.

"No shortage of abandoned construction sites around here. Walls to absorb the sound, and relatively private," Mac said, pushing all the ordnance on the floorboard around, so that none of the guns were pointing at him.

"But if we can get in, so can all the neighbors."

"Oh, Crank," The Bagman waved a finger. "'Stone walls do not a prison make.'"

"No. No, that's completely wrong. Stone walls make a great prison, ask the guys in stir."

"Then let's just take him out in the woods somewhere."

"And get shot by bootleggers?"

They were on their way to the woods to scare the truth out of him, when the little gangster sat up and started talking on his own.

"It wasn't me! I swear!" Before anybody could ask who did it, the kid said four words.

"It was the cops."

Chapter III
Doctor Death

Seven A.M. the next morning, Mac had skipped breakfast to stop by Crankshafts Car Repair on his way to work. He missed being able to drop by the graying mechanic's lot whenever he wanted to. He'd gotten little sleep the night before, and wanted to talk about the case.

Crankshaft, on the other hand, was already yelling.

"And you believe that? You think a bunch of Chicago cops drove out of town and murdered a waste of time like this Stinky guy?"

"You ever hear of a thing called the St. Valentine's Day Massacre, Crank? Besides, he didn't say cops. He said a cop—and all the guy did was flash a badge. Hell, you've seen me do that! He was hiding in the closet—terrified, for cryin' out loud."

"Yeah, maybe. I still don't think you should have let him go, though."

"Ah, you didn't see him yesterday morning. That kid thought Stinky was some kind of wizard or something. And did you see where he had us drop him off? Probably his parent's house."

"So it's like that Great Gatsby novel, he's one of those entitled rich kids that don't even see the harm his actions cause."

"He lives on the north side, Crank. Not Highland Park."

"OK. So then it could be anybody." Crankshaft shrugged.

"Yeah, the badge thing is child's play."

"Then you're the first one I'd suspect."

After a half-hour of bludgeoning each other with wit, the two agreed on one thing—the lack of blood. Meaning, Stinky had already been dead when somebody had blown his brains out.

Mac was starving, but he'd have to make do with a candy bar from the store. He normally stopped at a diner for breakfast, but he was already running late. Bundles of morning newspapers greeted him on the sidewalk in front of the shop.

The banner headline devouring the top half of The Sun read "Confession to Murder." Which would have been a typical headline for Mac to ignore, except for one thing—beneath it was a picture of Strother Cornbluth? Standing in the picture next to Cornbluth was a man in a suit, a Lieutenant Derek Martin of the Chicago Police Department. He was waving a piece of paper around; probably the boy racketeer-turned-murderer's confession.

Just glancing at the picture, Mac noticed the Cornbluth kid was leaning backward, trying to stay away from this Lieutenant Martin. He could see the fear in Strother's eyes, staring at the cop. Mac was about to cut the twine off the bundle and read the story when he heard a voice.

"Hey, mister, you're late." It was the tall, young man The Bagman had asked to call the fire engine the day before. He was wearing the same straw boater he'd had on yesterday and glancing at his watch. "Not that I'm complaining, but I got an appointment across town at nine."

Mac looked up at him blankly, said, "Oh." He picked up the bundle and remembered The Bagman had promised this guy ten bucks—but Mac wasn't supposed to know about that. After opening the door he said, "Man, you must really need a smoke, waiting for the store to open and everything."

"No, not really. It's just that—you know that bank robbery yesterday? That Bagman guy said if I called the Fire Department somebody at this store would pay me ten dollars."

"Ten dollars!" Mac's voice boomed. "Ten dollars?" He slapped the counter with a rolled up newspaper. "Look around the store buddy. I'd have to sell half my stock."

The man pulled the boater off his head like he was about to get in a fight and didn't want to break it. "So he lied? You don't even know the guy, do you?"

"Listen, Buddy. Nobody knows who that guy is. Anybody could just put a bag over their head and—"

"That's OK. I understand. You wouldn't happen to bank at First Chicago over there, would you?"

"Matter of fact, I do."

"Well, I was wondering, see." His fingers spun the hat around in his hands. "Since I kind of helped catch those robbers, if you think about it, I helped save your money. And I have to be downtown in less than an hour, I got a shot at a job, and I need cab fare."

Mac pretended to grumble as he made his way back to the cash register. He'd never intended not to pay his messenger. He just didn't want any connections drawn between him and The Bagman. He hit the cash register. It jingled and the drawer popped open. Suddenly, one of his eyebrows rose, and he looked up at the boyish-man.

"What kind of job you looking for?"

The man hesitated. "Well, I'm an artist, really—but my appointment's for a warehouse job."

"You sound like a pretty good salesman. Ever think about working in a cigar store?" Mac cut the twine off one of the bundles, and slid some newspapers into their rack.

"Truth is, I'd take anything, mister. But the warehouse is offering ten dollars a week."

"I'll give you twenty. Five day work week, but you'll have to work Saturday."

"I'll take it."

"What's your name?"

"Richie. Richie Cobb." He held out his hand, and they shook on it.

Before he had a chance to retrieve his palm, Mac had dropped the store keys into it.

"I'll be back before five. Treat yourself to a cigar if you want." He walked to the door and stopped after he opened it, looked back. "And if anything's missing when I come back, I will hunt you down and make you wish I'd killed you."

Richie's smile tugged straight, and his eyebrows lowered, even though he knew Mac was kidding—sort of.

Mac headed for the trolley thinking, Tough guy, eh. This might work.

The tough guy was still standing in the middle of the cigar store, staring at the keys in his hand, worrying about what would happen if he took a candy bar instead of a cigar.

❖ ❖ ❖

A few years back, during the Capone era, a reporter dropped by The Cook County Jail to interview a couple of felons. A secretary had informed him the two prisoners were not "available" at the moment—they had "an appointment downtown" and would "return after dinner." That Strother Cornbluth had been neglected such generous bond measures, was just another sign that Stinky Everett was no Al Capone. Heck, even Capone wasn't Capone anymore.

So it was with childlike excitement that Strother jumped off the edge off his metal bed when the guard told him "Your lawyer is here." Cornbluth had already spoken to the seemingly useless public defender, but he certainly wasn't going to turn down an opportunity to get out of an eight-by-ten cell.

Entering the visitor's room, Cornbluth's forehead furled with confusion. He didn't see his attorney. The guard pointed to a brawny looking man whose reddish handlebar mustache seemed only a little less bushy than his eyebrows. Cornbluth sat down, anyway.

"May I ask who you are, sir?"

"You don't know me, but I saw you the day before you got arrested. You were working a protection racket for Stinky Everett. You didn't kill him. Why'd you confess?"

"How do you know I didn't kill him?" Cornbluth snarled. "You think I couldn't do it?"

"No, I think you're too smart to do it. I also think you worked for Stinky because he talked you into it. So tell me, how'd you kill him?"

"It's all in my statement. I shot him in the back of the head," Cornbluth muttered, his face almost falling to the tabletop to rest in his hands.

"Then your statement's a lie, Strother, because a bullet in the head ain't what killed him."

"Who are you?"

"Somebody that wants to keep you from frying in the chair. I know you didn't do it," he said, as if he were placing a bet with himself. "That detective... Martin? The right hand man to our no-reform sheriff—he took a telephone book to your head, didn't he?"

"No. Listen mister, you better just go. You can't beat city hall, even I know that."

"Show me your hands."

"What?"

"Just show me the palms of your hands."

Cornbluth spread his fingers and put the palms of his hands up against the wire meshed glass that separated the two men. The guard two stalls away ran over and levered him back in his chair with a billy club. But he was too late; the man with handlebar had seen burn marks running across the palm of Cornbluth's hand; exactly like the ones on Stinky Everett's.

"Did he tell you if you didn't confess he'd kill you?"

Cornbluth's head spun back-and-forth as if he were afraid someone was listening. "Not just me," he whispered. "I can handle it, it's my parents..." His voice trailed off.

"So you don't mind dying, if it's for your folks." He smiled beneath the mustache. "Welcome to the rackets, Cornbluth. I may be able to help."

"Who are y—" But the brawny man was already walking away with his briefcase.

❈ ❈ ❈

Mac almost threw his nose away in the parking lot, but stopped when he remembered this was the second time he'd stocked up on the same face at the same theater supply. Then he remembered he'd used the same disguise to rob the 43rd precinct police of a small armory a few weeks ago. Never mind that he'd signed the visitor's log today as Lamont Cranston; it might be time to get a new disguise. He stepped into the souped-up Packard he'd taken off Crankshaft's lot, and put the nose and facial hair into a handkerchief. As he hit the street, he couldn't resist throwing it on the sidewalk, hoping all along some kid would find it and think somebody had blown their nose off.

He took the first left from the jail and headed for Cook County Hospital. Since he was in the area, he needed to talk to the one guy that could answer his questions.

One of the Cook County Coroner's newer doctors, Dexter Hayden was one of their

Cornbluth spread his fingers and put the palms of his hands up against the wire meshed glass that separated the two men.

best. In fact, he had helped The Bagman catch a murderer—and actually been nice about it. Mac hadn't even had to threaten him. The biggest problem was getting into the autopsy room to see Dexter. It was off limits except for doctors. Mac tried entering through the Emergency Room first, but they wouldn't let him in unless he was a patient. So he was forced to go into the building his least favorite way. The front door.

Upon entering, Mac was immediately confronted by a man behind a curved marble counter who asked "May I help you?"

"Oh, hi there. I'm here to visit Mr. Smith." Mac hadn't expected the questions, but surely there had to be a Mr. Smith in the hospital. There had to be.

"And what's his first name?"

"Strother." Mac bit his lip even as he was speaking. Cornbluth's name had just popped out, the first thing on his mind.

"I'm sorry, sir," the clerk said, thumbing through the log. "There's not a Strother Smith listed at the moment."

"Did I say Strother, I meant to say Joe. He hates being called Strother. In fact when he's not using his middle name, he uses a nickname."

"And what is that?"

Mac knew if he missed this one, he only had one more chance. "Joe."

"Ah, here we are. A Mister Joe Smith, room 234. Upstairs and to the left."

Mac nodded and strode toward the stairs. So there actually was a Joe Smith. Sounded like the kind of guy that could use a nickname.

When the man at the desk turned back around, Mr. Smith's visitor weaved from his path toward the stairway and around the corner. He strolled into of one of the labs, and before the door was back in place, he was exiting with a clipboard and a lab coat on. You could get anywhere with a clipboard and the right story. The lab coat on the other hand was a little too tight, but he found a dollar in the pocket and took that as a good sign. After that, nobody seemed to notice the big doctor as he blithely strolled to the back of the hospital where the dead men go.

Dexter Hayden was one of those people that loved his work. Which under any other circumstance would have been normal, except Dexter's job was cutting up dead people. A hard worker, the young doctor was only one Cook County Coroner, but he did the work of two. Hours seemed to just slide by for Doctor Hayden when he performed an autopsy, as if the rest of the world had simply disappeared.

When the young coroner returned to work after a late lunch, he didn't notice the extra hat hanging on the coat rack. He still had work on his mind, or at least bodies. One sat on a gurney, beneath the sheets, next to the wall—instead of in a drawer where it belonged. Somebody must've just rolled it in. And since the Cook County Coroner only handled high profile cases, he knew he better get to it. Dexter looked at his watch and pulled the gurney next to the autopsy table.

Picking up a scalpel, he turned and pulled the sheet off the body.

It sat up.

"How ya doing, Dex?" The faceless body asked.

Doctor Hayden jumped back four feet, holding the scalpel out to defend himself. Then he saw The Bagman.

"Holy cats! You almost scared the life out of me," Dexter spoke between gasps.

"Guess you'd fit right in down here then, huh?"

The coroner threw the knife in Mac's direction, not trying to hit him, but letting him know he meant business. "Don't! Ever! Do! That! Man, I almost stabbed you…" He was still shaking, running his fingers through his hair, but the words had force. Probably because the scalpel had stuck in the wall like part of a carnival act.

"Sorry about that, Doc. It's just I never know who's going to come walking in that door. Seemed best to kind of wait out of view."

"I've got an idea, why don't you just call first! I'll meet you in the parking lot."

"No can do, Doc. I got too many adoring fans out there… 'Course they all want to put a bullet in my head."

"Yeah, I can understand that. I saw in the papers how you took out a mob boss and blew up a bar since the last time I saw you. Take a tip from the Lone Ranger. Ride into town, then be smart enough to ride out. You'll live longer."

"Look, Doc. I know you love the Lone Ranger and all, but the last time I tried to ride a horse, it threw me on my head."

Dexter nodded, as if that explained everything. "So what do you want, Ranger? I got bodies piling up in my 'in box.'"

"Question: Two men, one dead, one near dead. Both of 'em had two thin lines on the palms of their hand, almost like a burn mark. There was some blistering, too. I'm thinking electrocution, but you're the expert. Is it possible?"

"Ah, the thin black line. Seen a couple of those, but our kind city fathers keep pulling 'em out of here before I can determine the cause of death—they've been telling me the cases aren't that important and then farming them out to friendly morticians. You say you have one dead, and one alive. Any difference in the burn marks?"

"Well, the dead guy's burn didn't look as bad as the one that's still alive. But the corpse had a hole in his leg."

"Exit wound. That's what happens with electric shock victims. All that energy has to go somewhere. What about the other guy?"

"Still alive. As far as I know there's no exit wound, but I'm not sure."

"Then he probably got hit by a lower voltage. High voltage boils your inside, not your outside. Then you get the exit wound."

"So, what, they're hooking 'em up to car batteries, or blowing the fusebox?"

"Probably not." Dexter picked up a clean scalpel, and began walking toward the wall where corpses sat in drawers like folders in a file cabinet. "My guess would be two different batteries, or maybe some sort of generator where you could adjust the power flow."

"One of those huge balls of wire and iron at the power stations?"

"Nah, More likely a small hand cranked job, kind of like you use to start a car…"

The Bagman stood silent for a moment. Then he walked over to the wall and yanked out the scalpel Dexter had thrown.

"Thanks, Kimosabe," he said, handing it back to the doctor. "See ya at the silver mine." And with his last Lone Ranger reference he grabbed his fedora off the coat rack.

"Hiyo," Dexter said, eyeing his clipboard and walking toward the wall stocked with bodies.

The young doctor pulled open the drawer, and Mac left, before he had to look at the body—still thinking Dexter was a lot tougher than he looked. Somehow the Doctor Hayden had figured out how to live with death, and keep his sense of humor. People are so weird, Mac thought, putting his mask in his pocket as he faced the wall so no one could see, never once reflecting on the fact that he was the one sneaking into autopsy rooms and wearing disguises.

Hopping back in Crankshaft's Packard, Mac sped to the north side. He parked in front of a Rexall Drug on Clark, changed two dollars for a roll of nickels, and headed for the phone booth in back of the store. He closed the door, the tiny light and the metal fan in the ceiling came on.

When he pulled the phone book open on the shelf, there were about twenty numbers for the last name Martin. He adjusted the mouthpiece, and hoped he didn't run out of nickels.

"Hello, is Lieutenant Martin there? This is Detective—" he put his hand over his mouth and mumbled a name "—from the precinct house."

The phone booth's tiny fan whirred, and a tiny voice buzzed from the earpiece.

"Oh, I'm sorry. I must've dialed a wrong number," Mac said. "Really? Your name's Martin, too? Well, what a coincidence."

He hung up and repeated the process thirteen times before he finally said, "Do you know what time he'll be in…? No, there's no need to take a message, I'll probably run into him at the precinct house. Thanks."

He picked up a pack of smokes and a Dime Mystery Magazine he hadn't ordered for the store, paying for it with twenty-five cents from the roll of nickels. Judging from the weirdoes menacing the scantily clad dame on the cover, it was no mystery who the bad guys in the magazine were. Mac felt the same way about Lieutenant Martin.

Back in the Packard, he steered his way toward the Lieter Building on State, and briskly strode into Sears & Roebuck, where he bought four summer coats on clearance. They looked awful, like they'd been left in the sun too long, but Mac didn't care about that. This was about function, not form.

After that he went to sporting goods. Ten minutes later, he'd pulled the Packard up to Sears' loading dock, and three employees loaded the back seat with wire cages. He dropped the four jackets off at a specialty tailor down the block, and promised the owner fifty bucks if he could finish the job in two hours.

Then Mac swung by the cigar store, so he could relieve his new employee, Richie Cobb. He slipped the kid another buck, told him to come back in the morning and closed the store ten minutes after the help had gone. The change in the register cashed out right, and nothing had exploded. Mac figured he might have a new employee.

The sun was setting in the distance by the time Mac pulled up at Navy Pier, over a mile of boardwalk situated on Lake Michigan, near the mouth of the Chicago River. While freight and passenger ship activity were down at the world-famous port, the World's Fair had brought in a whole new crowd—a crowd Mayor Ed Kelly wanted to keep happy and free from vermin.

Mac walked to the dry end of the pier, and stepped down into the sand. The lake sat a good forty yards off, beneath the boardwalk. Between the big man and the water, resting in the shadows against one of the wooden beams, were two men. Their sweaters were frayed with holes and, given the summer heat, they didn't seem to care. One of them wore an oily Greek sailor's hat, while the other's head remained bare.

A pudgy little rat terrier yapped and danced around Mac, as if happy to see him. He reached down and let the dog smell his hand before he rubbed around its ears. When he stopped the terrier began hopping at his legs again.

"Dog ain't for sale, mister," said one of the frayed men, looking up from his pipe.

"Oh, I don't want the dog."

Ten minutes later, three men who normally would have been working the docks, were unloading cages from the back seat of Mac's car and carrying them onto the pier.

Chapter IV
To Serve and Collect

"**N**o." Crankshaft said. He was good at saying it, and he always meant it.

He'd been excited when Mac had slid the car to a stop outside and run to the office, banging the screen door against the side of the shack the next morning. Crankshaft loved driving The Blue Streak. That car was his baby. Half the reason he'd agreed to go along on The Bagman's little adventures. The old vet would have taken the car out every night if he could. But, he'd already been through one war, and he knew the best way not to get killed was to be where the bullets weren't. And, he hated the idea of going to jail. He pulled hard on the cigar he was lighting, and blew a wave of smoke at Mac as he continued:

"There's no way, I'm going after a crooked cop out in the open. All he has to do is flash his badge and shoot whoever he wants. You trying to get us both killed?"

"C'mon, Crank," Mac was begging. "It'll give you something to tell all the little grand-crankies about someday. Seriously, I've got a plan."

"Like, 'someday I'm going to retire and open a cigar store?' You are aware that I've seen some of your plans in action before?"

"And you're still here to complain about it, right? As I recall, you said you had fun!"

"I was lying."

"C'mo-o-on, Crank." Mac held his two hands out together as if prayer might convince the mechanic. "I need a wheelman. All you gotta do is stay in the car and keep the engine running."

Crankshaft knew the plan would change. Hell, it was insane—it would have to. But the Blue Streak was still his baby.

And, Mac might need some help, too.

"OK, you got a driver."

❈ ❈ ❈

Mac borrowed the Packard again, having never really returned it, and spun around the corner to the cigar store. When he pulled up, Richie Cobb was waiting for him. Mac stepped out of the car, handed him the key. Told him to open the door and count out the register. He did both in a timely fashion and even called on Mac to count the drawer again because Cobb thought he was a nickel short. Mac dumped the last of his roll of nickels in the drawer, and told him it was balanced, now.

Then the big man strolled around the shop. He could see where Cobb had even straightened and dusted in between the shelves.

"Good job, Richie," Mac said. "Any trouble yesterday?"

"Well, I did have to put up the "back five minutes sign" to get something to eat. But I don't think I was gone too long."

"Good, because I'm going to need to take off right after the mail comes. I promise you, you'll have Saturday off, how's that?"

An hour and a half later, Mac dropped by the tailor's shop on State Street, then turned around and headed for Navy Pier. The wiry pipe-smoker in the Greek sailor hat came up from the shadows under the pier to meet him. Mac handed him the four tailored coats in a pile. The old man pulled one from the bunch and held it by the collar, running his fingers across the inside lining like he'd never seen a coat before.

"You guys gonna be able to pull off your end of the deal, Cap'n?" Mac pulled out a cigarette and searched his pockets for a match.

The old sailor pulled out a trench-lighter and offered Mac the flame, before firing up his own pipe. "Mister, for two-dollars a head, we'll pull all the ends off and tie 'em in a knot!"

"You guys just be waiting by the phone—and get there fast." Mac said. "As long as you're quick there's no way this thing can fail." The two men shook hands one more time before the man with the pipe trudged back into the shadows beneath the boardwalk.

Mac sped the Packard back by Lieutenant Martin's house, to check on his schedule. His car was there, so it was reasonable to assume he would still be working the late shift. His wife had sounded like something big might be going down tonight. Mac went home and took a nap. When he woke up, he went back to the store, gave Richie a key and told him to come back tomorrow. Five minutes later, he locked the joint up.

When he pulled into the lot at Crankshaft's Car Repair, the sun was closing in on the city's skyline.

If Chicago had a fuse, it was about to be lit.

Crankshaft and Mac parked down the street from Lieutenant Martin's house and sat in the shadows. Mac didn't have his mask on yet, and Crank was in his ever-present mechanic's coveralls, his goggles hanging over the bill of his cap. The Blue

Streak's reflective windshield shined the night back at itself, partially keeping the two men hidden. Even sitting with the windows open, they were down the street and out of view. Besides, they weren't doing anything.

"So if this guy doesn't go to work till midnight, why are we already here?" Crankshaft said, flicking his fingers at the car keys hanging out of the wooden dashboard.

"Because Lieutenant Martin is doing a whole different kind of work, Crank. He's a busy guy with a tight schedule, who can't miss a chance to make some poor slob confess to a crime he didn't commit."

"Or, because he's afraid he'll miss a payment. That Pierce Arrow in the driveway is brand new."

"Yeah, if there's one thing cops are lousy at, it's hiding money."

"Tell you what," Crankshaft said, pulling his flat cap down over his eyes and sliding down in the seat. "You keep an eye out and I'm going to try to catch ten or twenty winks here."

"Too late, old man. Here he comes."

Martin stepped from the front door to the large sedan, and backed out of the driveway. Crankshaft didn't start the engine until the crooked cop was already pulling away. The starter clicked. The engine hummed. The Blue Streak's lights were off as it glided behind the bright new Peirce. Crankshaft didn't bother to turn them on until Martin had already pulled around the corner.

"Hurry up, Crank. You're losing him."

"Not being seen is not the same as not being able to see."

"I can see just fine, I just don't wanna lose him!" Mac grabbed the dashboard. His head swiveled excitedly back and forth from Crank to the street ahead.

"If I lose him, it's going to be because I've got a bonehead in the passenger's seat distracting me."

Mac didn't say anything after that, but he kept pumping imaginary foot pedals and pulling on the dash like he could drive the car that way.

After some fifteen minutes, he said, "Hey, Crank, is it just me—or is he headed toward—"

"Niles Center. But that last left takes us away from the township." Crankshaft said, still hanging back at the last corner trying to avoid being seen. There wasn't enough traffic for him to hide behind.

"Waitaminute!" Mac said. "Remember when we were trying to find a place to question Cornbluth? I know exactly where this guy's headed. An abandoned construction site on the east side of the road, maybe a half mile down. Somebody laid out the concrete for the basement and walls, but the job had been cancelled."

Crankshaft pulled out slowly as the Lieutenant's headlights disappeared over the next hill. The Blue Streak came over the other side with its lights off, and pulled over behind a small thicket, a good two-hundred yards from the Pierce Arrow.

"Give him ten minutes," Mac said. "If he doesn't come out by then, I'm going in."

But two shapes came out of the darkness before any words could be traded. It was evident that Lieutenant Martin was shoving a handcuffed man across the small clearing, toward the Pierce Arrow. The prisoner fell down and Martin kicked him, before giving the man a hand back up, and kicking him again to keep him moving.

Once the two silhouettes were in the car, the trail led back to the city. Lieutenant Martin drove back to Chicago and parked behind the Central Division building on Twelfth Street. Crankshaft pulled past and kept the two men in his rear view mirror. After Martin led his prisoner inside the precinct building, the souped-up Graham Blue Streak parked on the street closer to the corner than the front entrance. Mac hopped out.

"Be right back, Crank." He pointed to the drug store across the street, where he was supposed to make a phone call.

Crankshaft settled back in his seat. This thing could take all night—and if it was anything like Mac's usual plans it would. The ace mechanic pulled his hat down over his eyes, crossed his arms and sat back awaiting Mac's return, still checking in the rear view mirror every once in a while. Ten minutes later he heard footsteps and a familiar voice.

"Heads up, Crank. Do something with this."

Mac slammed the passenger door. Crankshaft pushed the bill of his cap up just in time to see his friend holding up a large grocery bag, its top rolled up like a sack lunch.

"What the hell's that, a new mask?"

"Didn't I just tell you a little while ago, cops are lousy at hiding money?"

Crankshaft looked in top of the bag. It was full of cash, still stacked and wrapped in bands from the treasury. "Damn, Mac. This guy is filthy in more than one sense of the word."

"Yeah, well I got an idea while I was in the drugst—" An old Model-T truck had pulled up behind them. Mac glanced out the window, and opened the door. "Gotta go, Crank. Those are my guys. Keep your eyes open."

Crankshaft didn't bother to mention he'd been on watch while Mac was still in knickers. Meanwhile, Mac ran back to the Model-T. Two men who looked like unemployed dockworkers stepped outside and around the wooden bed of the truck, where Mac met two other salty but frayed-looking types lounging in the back.

"You all set?"

"Finally got 'em all stuffed in them coats, 'bout a half-hour ago," said the old salt with the pipe. "Barely got 'em all in, got to be at least a hundred. Way I figure it the fabric ain't gonna hold too long."

Mac shoved five twenties into the man's hand. "That's a hundred now, and a hundred after you guys do your voodoo."

The old salt put the cash in his pocket, and the two men stood staring at the police station, then back at the pile of clothing in the wooden bed of the truck. Their glances lingered only a moment.

One of the coats was twitching.

Chapter V
War of the Rats

Four grubby men walked into the lobby of the Second Precinct, Central Division. Two of them wandered toward the back corners, and two sat down on the long benches closer to the hallway that led to the officer's desks in back. The sergeant at the desk was too busy with the two A.M. crowd to even notice. If he had looked up from the crowd of people he was exchanging verbal barbs with, he might have noticed something odder than even the four ragged men wearing long coats on a summer night.

For instance, he might have noticed that whatever those coats were lined with was awfully thick. Or that all the men, especially the ones sitting down, looked as if they were holding the coat's lining away from themselves. And if he had bothered to pay even momentary attention, there was no way he could have missed the fact that the bottom of the coats were stricken with spasms.

Mac walked into the center of the room with his hat pulled down over his charcoal smeared face. He was about to give the signal when one of the raggedy men in the corners stood up and screamed. When the lady next to him saw the rat's head pop out of the coat's lining, she screamed, too. For a second stone silence cut through the room—then the crowd exploded.

All the men in long jackets stood, yanking at cords connected to the lining of their coats. The entire waiting room flooded with vermin. Rats, mice, even roaches, all scattered for the walls in a wave, skittering through the room and into the halls.

Teeny herds of bug-infested varmint fur washed over their feet like clouds of mangy hair. Both men and women kicked in reflex, and gray furry balls flew through the air before others got stomped into crimson mush. Hands flew to their hair and faces. The sergeant at the desk drew his service pistol like he was going to start shooting. Everybody else made for the exits.

Except Mac.

The big man marched swiftly down the hall where the detectives were stationed. He'd tried to find the blueprints for this place, but simply hadn't had the time. He was running on hunches. The hunches led him past the holding cells and the prisoners.

The guard running up front to see what all the commotion was about didn't feel Mac grabbing the large key ring off his uniform belt. Mac skipped any of the criminals who might've been a real danger, but when he reached the drunk tank he couldn't help himself. He unlocked the gate and some twenty, very odd customers exploded into the hallway. Mac stood behind the cell door, then headed in the other direction. Downstairs.

The entire hallway was concrete. Lit by bare bulbs in cages on the ceiling, the mint-colored walls were powerless against the dank air and hopelessness of the place. The doorways that led to interrogation rooms seemed even scarier. Mac headed for the door that felt the worst.

The wire-reinforced window in the wall had the blinds closed. Mac couldn't help the feeling that there was something back there nobody was supposed to see. Security only a cop would fall for, he thought. The Bagman pulled the mask on over his head and wedged it into place with his hat. Then he kicked the door open.

He had been expecting something bad, but actually seeing it made him stop.

Two men in suits, Lieutenant Martin and another detective, stood over their victim. Seated in the room was a man tied a wooden chair with his feet in a bucket. There were cigarette burns, and straight black burn marks on his chest. His hand quivered and the wires he held slid out of his hand. The two wires led to a small wooden box about a foot square with a brass crank handle on the side. For a second Mac thought the man was dead.

Lieutenant Martin went for his gun. The Bagman took a step to the detective's right and kicked him in the stomach. Martin pulled the trigger. But The Bagman grabbed the gun by the top, wedging the chamois-cloth skin between the thumb and forefinger of his glove between the hammer and the firing pin.

Mac didn't want to draw any attention now that he was here, but when he jerked his hand back and the gun came clamped to it, he wailed. It echoed off the concrete walls and down the hall. He pulled the hammer back, and yanked the gun off like a mousetrap had been clamped on his hand. The inside of his glove turned warm and wet with blood. When The Bagman looked back up again, his eyes were glowing like molten steel.

The detective next to the lieutenant had his gun out and Mac was in his sights. Mac threw Martin's pistol at the man's head, to foul his aim. The detective ducked.

In time too fast to measure Mac took a step closer.

"Freeze, killer. You're under arrest," the cop said. "Drop your gun."

The Bagman's feet stopped moving, but he didn't quite freeze. He didn't reach for his shoulder holster and drop his gun, either. Instead he stood, unmoving with his feet apart. He twisted his head as if his neck hurt.

"Don't even think about it," the detective said.

One of The Bagman's shoulders rolled forward. He flicked his wrist and eighteen inches of iron rebar slid into his hand from where it had been taped to his arm. There was a blur and the cop's wrist was broken. Before he could scream, it glanced off his head and he crumpled to the floor.

He'd been lucky. Mac was aiming at his teeth.

The Bagman scanned the room, cursing under his breath. He hadn't planned on the torture victim being quite so...tortured. He pulled his mask off, and threw Lieutenant Martin over his shoulder in a fireman's carry. Then he picked up the wooden box by the crank with one hand, wrapped that arm around the lieutenant's legs, and grabbed the torture victim by the wrist with his other arm. He dragged the wounded man out into the hall in hopes that one of the good cops would find him.

There had to be one.

With the wooden box under one arm, Mac pulled his hat down over his face, and made for the stairs to the rear exit—all this while still carrying Lieutenant Martin over his other shoulder so nobody could see who he was. The original plan had been to use the side exit next to the lobby, but there was no way The Bagman was going to walk through the mayhem upstairs unseen. He kicked the rear exit open, expecting to have to run around the building. Damned if the Blue Streak wasn't idling right there in front of him.

Crankshaft had his reflective goggles on. In the coveralls he looked like some kind of moon man, smiling and revving the engine.

Mac shoved the detective into the back of the two-seater's cab, blocking the rear view, and then climbed into the car. He wasn't going to chance either of them riding in the rumble seat.

Crankshaft floored it. Mac waved out the window at the rat-catchers, glad to see they were all right, but still trying to hide his face. He'd have to pay them the rest of their money tomorrow. Heck, as far as he was concerned those guys were scarier than the cops any day.

Speeding for the north side, the Blue Streak's engine purred. Mac pulled a roll of masking tape out of the glove compartment and pulled his bloody glove off with his teeth. Wiping the blood off, he could see where Martin's gun had ripped a half-inch of tissue out of the soft flesh on the inside of his thumb. He wrapped the tape around his hand, then turned around and wrapped the rest of it around the Lieutenant Martin's eyes and mouth until he looked like the invisible man, except his nose was sticking out.

It was going to hurt when The Bagman ripped all that tape off the crooked cop's head. Mac might even have been smiling.

Chapter VI
Bucket of Brains

He couldn't move his hands.

"That cold hard thing next to your head is a pair of scissors," the voice said. "You may not want to move your head."

Lieutenant Martin was blind and his whole body shaking. He flinched under the wad of tape around his head.

"Or, you might be happy with just one ear, I dunno…"

The lieutenant felt fingers like steel cables force themselves under the tape. One of the big hands grabbed a handful of his hair; the other one wrenched the shell of masking tape from his head. Martin made a moaning sound before his mouth could speak. "You're breaking my neck," he gasped as if he couldn't breathe. His eyes

He kicked the rear exit open, expecting to have to run around the building. Damned if the Blue Streak wasn't idling right there in front of him.

stayed clenched shut. One of the big hands slapped his face just hard enough to get the circulation going again. Lieutenant Martin winced.

"Jeez, you're just a big chicken, aren't you, copper?"

If Lieutenant Martin had bothered to look, he would've seen Crankshaft rolling his eyes in the background. The ace mechanic hated it when Mac talked like the pulp gangster version of Edward G. Robinson. And when Mac was The Bagman, he talked like that a lot.

They had brought the Lieutenant underground to the Secret Subway, the garage underneath Crankshafts Car Repair. Mac and Crankshaft had built a small toolshed in one of the corners to store all their equipment, both legal and illegal, just weeks ago. Tonight, they'd removed everything from the shed but a table and two chairs. The table was laden with all sorts of sharp scary-looking tools, and the ominous shape of the crank generator's wooden box beneath a sheet. Lieutenant Martin didn't know where he was.

Slowly, the lines on his eyes became shallower. He opened his eyes, shaking his head. Then looked up into a blank face, no mouth, no nose—just two steely eyes, made all the more mean-looking by the evil V the brows formed above them.

"Oh, Looey, what are we gonna do with you?" The masked man said, rhetorically. "Copper, copper, copper…"

Crankshaft was practically going into convulsions, his eyes rolling and his fist banging on the wall.

It startled the lieutenant. He spun his head from one man to the other, yanking at his bonds the entire time. Then he suddenly just stopped. He stared at his shoes, before he inhaled, exhaled, and finally looked up again.

The Bagman was holding up a bucket of water.

Lieutenant Martin started shaking again. "Nothin'! I ain't tellin' you nothin'!"

"Man alive." The Bagman slapped his thigh. "For a guy who's supposed to know how to interrogate a suspect, I thought you'd come up with something a little more original than that. What's the matter, cop, you forget what the bucket of water's for? Oh wait, I forgot—you're not a real cop. You're Torquemada. Heck, I'm willing to bet you're not even that bad, probably more of a Marquis De Sade. Gets you all tingly down there causing all that pain, doesn't it?" The Bagman poured the bucket of water on Lieutenant Martin's lap. "Probably a real release for ya, when they confess to something you actually did, huh?"

Martin spat at him, but his mouth was too dry.

Mac dumped the water in his lap. "Ve haff vays uf making you talk!" he said, and almost breaking into a satirical goosestep.

Crankshaft sat down in the other chair, again turning his head to and fro, tsk-tsking, probably more at Mac than at the lieutenant.

"An empty bucket ain't gonna hurt me none," Martin said.

Mac put the bucket on the lieutenant's head, and started banging on it with a lead pipe from the table. Lieutenant Martin screamed.

"Aaaaagh! That hurts."

Mac stopped. Stood with the hand holding the pipe on his hip, leaning back as if to get a better look at the situation. Lieutenant Martin's breathing slowed, calming down. Mac started banging on the bucket again.

"Aaah! Aaah! Aaah!" Martin stopped screaming when he couldn't breathe anymore.

"Yeah, you're right cop. Without the water that buckets's useless." The Bagman glanced over at Crankshaft and took the bucket off the lieutenant's head, then held it in the air by its wire handle. "I'll be back in a minute. I need more water," and he traipsed through the doorway so that all the captive Martin could see was the darkness outside.

Crankshaft rested one leg upon the other and sighed: "You know he's crazy, don't you?"

"What's that say about you? You—" He glared up into the mechanic's reflective goggles, "—you Martian, you!"

"Wow, are you stupid," the Martian said, picking something out of the tread of his boot. "I might be able to get you out of this thing alive," he chuckled. "I mean, I don't know if he's going to kill you or not. I may not be able to keep him from killing you—hell, if you do get out of here alive, it probably won't be what you call living. So why don't you just confess, or sign, or whatever the hell it is he wants you to do, and I'll try to make sure whatever it is, he does it as quickly as possible."

The crooked detective clenched his jaw and stared daggers at the black man. "If he's really crazy, why you hang around?"

"Somebody has to keep him under control. Seriously, he's happy right now, but you should see him when he's angry. It's horrible what he does to those kids."

"Kids?"

"Yeah. Kids and puppies. It's just horrible…" Crankshaft waggled his head some more.

The door behind him opened and slammed, again. The Bagman set the bucket of water next to the lieutenant's feet, and then unveiled the electric generator like a magician releasing a dove. He picked up the wooden box, holding the two wires extended from his left hand with the exposed ends crossed in the air, then cranked it once, hard. Sparks flew.

"OK, OK, I'll talk." The lieutenant wiggled against his bonds.

The Bagman tossed a Big Chief notebook and a pen on the side of the table nearest the detective. "Now you're talking. Write it all out, and sign."

Martin struggled at his bonds, his palms outward like he was trying to shrug his shoulders.

"You right or left handed?" The Bagman said, picking up a machete from the table.

The lieutenant's eyes clenched near shut, trying to block the horror out. "Right. I'm right handed."

The machete slammed against the right side of the chair. Martin raised his hand, surprised to see it was still connected to his arm.

"Look, I'll confess to anything you want, but you guys gotta know, I'm not the man in charge."

"Well, hell, cop. We already knew that. You think we actually believed you were smart enough to pull this off by yourself?" The masked man picked up a straight razor and started sharpening it on the leathery strop connected to the table. "You just tell us who that ol' evil mastermind is—and we'll make sure it's all over easy for you."

Lieutenant Martin swallowed, looking around the room for a sign of hope. Crankshaft nodded slowly to him behind The Bagman's shoulder. The lieutenant reached with his free hand for the notebook with the pen on it, tugged them into place, and started writing. It was quiet for a moment before he signed his statement with a flamboyant gesture, looked up and said:

"Honest to God, guys. I didn't know nothing about this when I signed on to the BTF," Martin said.

"BTF?" The Bagman said.

"Yeah, the Bagman Task Force. Orders came down from Mayor Kelly, after you took out Slots Lurie."

"Bagman Task Force?" Both captors said in unison, turning to look at each other.

"The Kelly-Nash machine must've missed some of their dirty money, too..." Crankshaft mulled. "'Course with nobody paying taxes that's the only way the city can afford anything, I suppose."

"Justice is not this complicated." The masked man grabbed the lieutenant by the collar, and pulled him into the air with the chair still tied beneath him. "Who's in charge of this task force, the alderman?"

"No, no," Martin stammered. They brought in some undercover cousin of Kelly's, some kid named Cobb."

"Richie Cobb?" The eyes behind the mask went wide.

"Yeah, that's it. He was supposed to live in the neighborhood, call us out whenever you were sighted. He looks innocent, but the kid's all strategy. He was tellin' us where exactly to be, and what kinda' guns to carry. Meanwhile, he came up with this plan to keep arrests up and keep the money flowing."

The Bagman's teeth clenched, and then twisted into a grin only the Devil could love. He shoved the exposed wires into the lieutenant's neck, and shoved the crank on the generator down. Lieutenant Martin yelped and bounced out of the seat, his mouth wide open. The Bagman shoved the sleeping pills he'd gotten at the drugstore into the dirty cop's throat, and massaged them down with the palm of his hand like he was giving medicine to a dog.

"Richie Cobb? Isn't that the name of the kid you hired?"

"IF that's his real name. He's not an artist—he's a con artist." Mac picked the lead pipe back up and slammed it in the palm of his hand. "Crank, ya wanna go to work with me today?"

Chapter VII
Criminal Justice

Richie Cobb showed up at Mac's Tobacco a little after eight that morning. He hung around in front of the store for a while, waiting to see if Mac would show up. Finally, he opened the door with his key and pulled the morning papers inside, noticing somebody had cut the twine on one of the bundles. A copy of the Tribune was missing. He made a note of it, then went in back and counted out change for the register at exactly nineteen dollars and ninety-nine cents, before he turned the sign in the window around where it read "OPEN, come on in."

He was sitting behind the register eating a Charleston Chew and reading the Tribune's headline—Rats Invade Police Station—when the tiny bell hanging on the door sounded announcing the first customer of the day.

"Morning, sir, how can ahuuh—" Cobb's tongue flopped over his lip like he'd just gotten a shot of Novocain. "Y—you're him!"

The Bagman was standing in the doorway with his fedora pulled down and the brim snapped at eye level. Stepping in from Lincoln Avenue with the sun behind him, he looked like he'd just stepped out of a western movie. The only way to describe him was… big. Not fat, not eight-feet tall. It was something beyond physical. It was something about the mask and the blue steel burning in his eyes, something almost evil. He just stood there, and all that weirdness oozing off him filled the room.

"Funny thing about the Trib this morning," The Bagman said, slapping a rolled up newspaper in his palm like he had the lead pipe. "They didn't mention the rats on the north side."

Richie Cobb swallowed and began to edge slowly back toward the stockroom. "Look, mister, I dunno what you want, but whatever it is, just take it. This ain't even my store."

"I wasn't talking about the store, dimwit. I was talking about my neighborhood." The Bagman's voice cut through the air, not loud, but imperative. "I heard it was because you're a cousin of somebody in Mayor Kelly's machine."

Cobb's hand swiped for the inside of his coat. The Bagman slapped him upside the head with the rolled up newspaper—back and forth—fast and hard. The Tribune was a thick daily, and by the time Cobb had gotten around to touching his gun, it was gone. When he shook his head and looked up, his gun was twirling on The Bagman's index finger.

The masked man grabbed him by the hair while his other hand swept across Cobb's body, looking for a knife. Cobb didn't resist. The Bagman found the knife, took the wallet. What he didn't find was a badge.

"So you're not undercover?" The Bagman let go of Cobb's hair, slinging him away.

"No. I just got this job here."

"Liar… First of all, if you're telling the truth your eyes don't shift both ways when you're telling it. Plus, I talked to a guy who knows a guy, and then kidnapped another guy. And they must have told me the truth—because they're still alive," the man with no face said, sounding like one of the neighborhood mooks. It looked like he was smiling under the mask, but he could have been gritting his teeth, you couldn't tell.

Cobb's knees were shaking. Every false step he made for the back door made him look squirrelier. He jumped, gasping when the door behind him thumped shut.

A wiry black man in an oil-stained jumpsuit blocked the exit. He had eyes like a fly and was holding a wooden box in hands. It was about a foot-square, with a brass crank handle on the side.

Cobb leapt sideways like the box was on fire. The man with no eyes set the box on the counter and pointed a U.S. Army Automatic from the World War at him.

The Bagman hadn't even seemed to notice. He was still thumbing through Richie's wallet when he said:

"You shouldn't 've jumped like that, Cobb. Means you know what that box is for." There was a long pause. The Bagman was still going through the wallet. "And you should never leave a card in your wallet with a list of dirty cops' names and numbers on it." He ripped a card out and held it in the air, pointing at it with his other hand. "Hey, is that the mayor's personal phone number?"

Cobb was all but whimpering in the corner.

"Y'know, I can understand calling the police if you're in danger, or if you think somebody else might be. But for the life of me… No, not the life of me. How many men have you tortured to death? Do you know how many men you've sent to the chair? Or to prison? Innocent citizens?" He glared down at Cobb, who was sobbing on the floor. "And don't give me that crap about the ends justifying the means, either—'cause I've been living that one and the means just get dirtier and meaner."

The Bagman grabbed Cobb's straw hat off the rack, stepped toward him and offered it as if he were taking him for the proverbial ride. Cobb wilted, but took it and put it on his head.

The masked man grabbed him by the throat, and forced three sleeping pills down his gullet. Cobb passed out like he'd been hit over the head.

"Now we have two unconscious men on our hands," Crankshaft said. "You let them go, they're just going to come back and kill you. We're talking about cops here. Are you willing to kill them?"

"Stop being so cynical, Crank. It's people like you that make this Depression so damned depressing." Mac eyed Lieutenant Martin. He couldn't believe the guy had just passed out. "And, no, I'm not gonna kill 'em. Remember how I knew about the construction in those woods outside Niles Center? Well, there's a reason I know about the woods out there. Couple of guys I know run a still about a half-mile away. You might want to bring a bottle to fill, too. They make a mean corn mash."

Crankshaft eyed him sideways. They picked up Cobb's unconscious body by the hands and feet, took him out the backdoor, and loaded him in the back of the truck they had borrowed from the Car Repair.

❀ ❀ ❀

When Lieutenant Derek Martin first woke up his head hurt.

He was tired. Couldn't seem to lift his head, but he kept trying to wake up. Somebody poured some liquor in his mouth. He coughed and opened his eyes. Closed them and fell back asleep again. He was so tired.

Forcing his eyes open, he realized he didn't know where he was. His arms felt like anvils– dead, heavy weight. Wait a minute, he thought, this is the construction site. The one he kept prisoners in, while the boss decided what to do with them. How did he get back here?

The lieutenant heard something moan in the shadows, on the concrete in the opposite corner. *It was Special Detective Richie Cobb! What the hell were the two of them doing here? OhmyGod! The Bagman! He's gonna kill us!*

Lieutenant Martin concentrated on moving, but his arms just flopped at his sides. A flashlight beam cut through the scrubby wooded darkness, then another. *He's coming to kill us. He'd have to...*

Martin tried to move again. His whole body felt numb. There was something in his hands. Floodlights exploded over the construction site, exposing every tiny twig. Then he heard a siren. *The cops! It's the cops! Oh, thank you, thank you, thank you, thank you! I'm safe! Clean and safe!* Martin shook his head, trying clear it.

"Here they are! Over here!" A uniformed policeman stared down at him from above, about twenty feet from the abandoned building's foundation. He pulled his gun, one eye staring down the barrel.

Cobb noticed something shiny in his peripheral vision.

He started to turn his head, but before his neck could respond, he already knew what it was. He could smell it. A still. The damn thing was smoking. Somebody was distilling corn whiskey, here in the middle of the woods.

Oh, no, wait a minute, he tried to say. *I'm a cop, too!* That's when he remembered they weren't Chicago Police, but Niles Center. *God he was so tired, he had to...*

Two of the policeman stood directly in front of him, two in front of Richie Cobb.

"I think this one's drunk," one of the policemen said.

"This one, too" said the sergeant. "Prohibition ain't over yet, brother! Book 'em!"

Somebody else started talking fast. Something popped, and even more light flashed.

A flash bulb! Reporters!

Lieutenant Derek Martin looked down at his hands, remembering something had been in them. His left hand lay next to a gallon jug of corn mash. When he finally forced his right hand up in front of his face, there was a piece of paper from a notebook stuck between his fingers.

He recognized his signature as the sergeant tore it out of his hands.

THE END

Chicago, We Have a Problem...

So I'd just finished my book TALES OF THE BAGMAN. I'd sent it in to my trusty editors—drafted, redrafted, and edited their edits so they could re-edit mine—when I got an e-mail in my box that said, "I need another BAGMAN story!" And of course, I quickly wrote back "no problem."

Of course, there was a problem. The next BAGMAN book was forming in my head and involved the Chicago World's Fair of 1933, possibly more than 150 pages, and possibly more than one villain—and I'd hardly started researching.

So, the first thing I did was pick up the continuity. Mac was now supposed to be running a Cigar Store, which was a great ending for the first book, but not the best place to pick up the next story. I had originally figured managing a cigar-store would be the perfect job for Mac, until I started writing this story. First of all, it kept Mac from hanging out with his pals—and let's face it, that's where the action is. Second, I realized Mac's just not a customer service kind of guy. Sure, relatively normal pulp heroes like The Crimson Mask can work in a drugstore, or The Avenger can consult with one of a hundred different companies, but Mac? He'd be bored to death. So, in one sentence Mac's Tobacco ceased to be a legitimate business and became a front. I had no idea that was going to happen when I started this story, but The Bagman's just too much of an operator to be tied down behind a counter selling smokes and Jujubes.

And then, to top it all off, I realized I had to introduce the character to readers who may have yet to read the astonishing tales presented in The Bagman's debut. And I suddenly realized why there wasn't always a lot of continuity in the old pulp hero yarns. It ain't easy to do.

So I simply started doing. I didn't have a villain yet, but that didn't matter, I simply had to start with some action. Well, my brain said, how about Mac foils a bank robbery to start things off? Perfect, I said to my brain, and proceeded to nail down ten pages of the most hard boiled, gangbusting violence any mind in the Western world could comprehend.

And it simply didn't work. It didn't feel right. Because, while Chicago's favorite masked mental case would protect the neighborhood, he wouldn't necessarily go in guns blazing like a billion other masked mystery men. No, Mac is all about saving the neighborhood and then the world. He wouldn't want to risk the stray bullets, or the death of a hostage. He'd be clever.

And that's how I proceeded to write the only heroic pulp tale I know of, where the hero runs away from the action in order to double cross the bad guys. Yup, Mac is definitely different. Dangerously different, kinda' clever, and all kinds of weird.

My hero.

So while I was redrafting the beginning and still looking for a villain, the real world fell onto my head, a local news story that could only bring fertile life to the twisted darkness that makes this writer so happy. Former Chicago Police Department Detective and Commander, John Burge was convicted of torturing hundreds of criminal suspects between 1972 and 1991. Burge was accused of beatings involving cattle prods, violet wands, and a small wooden box, similar to an old telephone crank, that was used to shock the face and inner thighs of its victims (remember the movie *Brubaker*? same thing). And for my money, just looking at the guy, he was immediately emblazoned—no, make that scarred—into my consciousness as a villain.

So, while I didn't want to do another crooked cop story. I had to.

For me the entire concept of torture is not only dehumanizing for every party involved, it is also induces the sort of terrified, helpless feeling no human should ever have to endure. It is a concept that is ultimately so appalling that I can't stand to see it used in popular entertainment. I shouldn't have to be conditioned to torture to be scared by it. So yeah, even on a good day, I'm still pretty repulsed by the whole humans-hurting-humans thing. Probably why I love heroes so much.

Regarding Chicago's corrupt Mayor Ed Kelley… well, he was corrupt. And while I like to keep these yarns somewhat historically accurate, I have no problem nailing Kelly or the Cook County Sherriff of the time as crooks either. They really did let mobsters take "field trips" from jail and their scams are now a matter of public record. Mac may be forced to have a few words with him in the future.

As long as I'm at it, the Babe Ruth Pocketknife is real too. The words in italics are a shortened version of the original ad. The information about the city of Skokie should all be valid other than Stinky's residence.

As far as loading a herd of vermin into a trench coat, I still haven't quite worked that one out, but I'm willing to bet the old rat catcher's used sail cloth. I'm probably not going to try this one at home, though. Regardless, if you're new to The Bagman— Welcome! We're just getting started. And if you're one of those lucky readers now on their fourth Bagman story? Well, hang around, some of those question marks have answers written in bullets, and more of the mystery is soon to be revealed!

Thanks, and remember, the world needs heroes—go be one!

B. C. Bell
Chicago, Nov. 2010

Author Bio

A lifelong pulp fan, B.C. Bell is the author of *TALES OF THE BAGMAN*, the novel which precludes this story. He has also written adventures for several different *AIRSHIP 27* titles including *SECRET AGENT X, Vol. 2, JIM ANTHONY SUPER-DETECTIVE*, and *DAN FOWLER G-MAN*. He currently has more pulp and a horror novel in the works. He lives in Chicago. Follow the adventures of both The Bagman and Bell on the *Tales of The Bagman blog* at http://chicagobagman.blogspot.com/ or join him on Facebook.

You can read his award winning short horror story, "How Pappy Got Five Acres Back and Calvin Stayed On the Farm over at SFReader.com for free!

THE RED VEIL

"Hell Hath No Fury..."

By Aaron Smith

"**A**lice, Alice, come out of there! You haven't eaten in days! Have you been sleeping or are you still crying? Come on out, child. At least let me know if you're alive in there!"

There was no reply for many minutes. Still Julia Carter waited outside the door. She was at her wit's end but after three days of her own mourning was beginning to feel her strength returning. As her own grief began to subside, though it was far from vanishing, her thoughts turned to concern for her daughter-in-law and she desperately wished the door would finally open.

The old hinges creaked and the knob turned. Julia Carter gasped with worry as the face appeared in the open doorway. Alice looked horrible, her hair a mess, nightgown wrinkled, face streaked with the lines made by tears cried over the course of nearly seventy-two hours alone, and her body still trembling as if trying with all its might to keep the shaking sobs from coming back.

"I'm…I'm sorry Mrs. Carter," she said, her voice shaking. "I…I didn't mean to worry you…but I just can't…I don't know what to do!"

Seeing the younger woman near collapse, exhausted, half-starved, overcome with sorrow, her mother-in-law wrapped her arms around her, trying to soothe or comfort her. She thought back a decade to when she had lost her dear William and knew that she had at least some sense of what poor Alice was going through. Still, she thought, William had gone peacefully after a valiant battle with the illness that had eventually taken him away from her. Alice had had no time to prepare, for poor Tommy, Julia's son, had been a sudden victim of a heinous act of violence, a far too frequent occurrence on the streets of the darker corners of the city. Julia could hardly imagine what it must have been like to have the love of one's life suddenly, unexpectedly, and permanently snatched away by a hail of bullets and ruthlessness. Tommy had been her son and she had nearly collapsed when the news had come, but she had seen death before and lived through it. Alice, on the other hand, was young, seemed fragile like a piece of fine porcelain, and could hardly be expected to bear the burden of such heavy grief at such a young age.

"I know it hurts dear, I know. I miss Tommy too, but he wouldn't want you to lock yourself away like this. You need to keep up your strength; the funeral is tomorrow. Now go and take a hot bath while I fix us some supper, Alice. And please, dear, won't you start calling me Julia? You're all I have now that my William and my poor little Tommy are gone. There's no need to keep calling me Mrs. Carter."

Alice pushed her mother-in-law away, took a deep breath to steady her nerves, and walked away into the bathroom, shutting the door behind her. When she emerged an hour later, her face was clean, long hair brushed, and some of the color had returned to her face. She still shook a bit, but the hot water and the steam had calmed her somewhat. She felt her hunger now, some of her grief-given numbness beginning to subside. She went back into the room she had spent the last three days in, the room that had belonged to Tommy when he had been a little boy, and got dressed. She tried her best to drive her terrible sadness deep down within herself and keep it there, at least for the evening. She knew that Julia was hurting too, now a mother without her child, and she realized that it would be selfish to continue to grieve in solitude. Julia had been right, Alice knew; they had each other now and that was all they each had. They would have to be each others' strength and spirit. Alice finished dressing, dabbed some makeup on her face to at least give the illusion that she felt like being alive, and went downstairs to be greeted by the smell of pot roast, mashed potatoes, onions, and hot bread. The scent increased her hunger and she walked more quickly into the dining room to join her mother-in-law at the freshly set table.

The food was excellent. Alice could tell that Julia had put her best effort into the preparation, probably glad to have something to do, anything to take her mind off of the loss they had both suffered. As they ate, Julia spoke of her son, telling Alice stories of Tommy's boyhood mischief. They both shed a few tears and shared a few smiles. When the main course was gone and the coffee consumed too, Alice stood up and walked towards the door.

"Mrs. Carter...Julia...I need some air. I'm going for a walk. I won't be gone long."

"Nonsense, Alice," Julia Carter responded. "I know exactly where you're going, because I'd do the same if I were you. You're going to walk over to your and Tommy's apartment and go inside and look at Tommy's things for the first time since you came here after you got the news that he was gone. And when you get there, you're going to miss him even more, but I won't tell you not to go; you'll have to go sooner or later I suppose. When you need me, Alice, I'll be right here waiting for you...and praying for the both of us."

Alice Carter left the little house where her beloved Tommy had grown up. It was a warm spring evening and she hadn't bothered to even bring a sweater. If she felt chilly, her clothes were mostly still at her own apartment; she'd brought only a small case with her when she'd gone to stay with her mother-in-law. As she walked along the streets in the mostly quiet, residential section of the city, her mind kept repeating her memories of the night, three days earlier, when her world had suddenly fallen off a cliff into the deepest pit of despair she could have imagined.

She had been home awaiting Tommy's arrival after she had spent the day shopping. He had made a little bonus money the month before for working a few extra shifts to cover for a friend who had been ill. Tommy took overtime whenever he could get it as the young couple had been trying to get ahead on some bills and stay up to date on the rent. Cops didn't make much, especially young patrolmen like Tommy Carter, but they got by. The extra overtime had brought in more money than usual and Tommy had insisted that Alice treat herself to a new dress. She had done so and had gone straight home and put it on to show Tommy when he got home from walking his beat. She couldn't wait to see his reaction to the way she looked in what she had selected for herself. They had been married just a few short years and still saw in each other that radiant glow that only the recently wed can perceive.

She was admiring her new dress in the bedroom's full length mirror when the knock on the apartment door had come. She glanced at the wall clock; shortly after seven, about an hour too early for Tommy to be home. She wondered who it was and walked to the front hallway of the apartment to answer the knock.

"Larry," she said, seeing a well known face in the doorway. "Sorry, but you're too early. Tom isn't home yet and even if he was…he's all mine tonight; there's no way I'm letting you take him out for a beer!"

Officer Larry Epstein had held his hat over his heart and hung his head in sadness as he muttered "Alice…I'm sorry." And Alice Carter had known that something had happened, that her dear Tommy had been taken from her.

Epstein told her what was known at that point as they both choked back sobs of loss. A call had been made reporting gunshots in a building on Tommy's beat. A patrol car had made its way to the area to investigate. Officer Thomas Carter had been found dead in an unrented third-story apartment, having succumbed to two shots to the chest. No arrest had been made, no suspects had been questioned, and no witnesses reported anything other than hearing the shots.

Alice had collapsed into a shaking and weeping puddle of grief and Officer Epstein had escorted her to the home of Julia Carter where the two of them had broken the news to the slain policeman's mother. Alice had stayed with the elder Mrs. Carter for the three days since Tommy's tragic death, his murder.

Now Alice walked the familiar streets of her neighborhood, aware of where she was but drifting in and out of the trance of numb disbelief that had been her home for the past three days. She had no tears left to cry and her slim body could stand no more trembling. She just walked, slowly and deliberately, knowing that she had to, sooner or later, face her return to an empty apartment, a set of rooms that would remain empty, at least empty of the presence of the man she had loved with more of her heart than anyone she had ever met before in her young life.

The sky had grown dark as she had slowly walked along those streets but Alice paid little attention to the coming of night. It had seemed, from her painfully grieving point of view, to have been the darkest of nights since she had heard the awful news of Tommy's death. It didn't occur to her to think that the streets in her neighborhood were not the safest of places during the late hours. She took a shortcut through a side street and squinted to see her way through the shadows cast by the walls of the two buildings that stood tall and proud on either side of her. She heard a noise, the clicking of shoes on hard concrete. Then a voice, rough and not entirely sober, came from the darkness in front of her. As the light of some upper-story lamp just managed to penetrate the shadows, she saw a face before her. It was a scruffy face, unshaven and tough; no gentleman stood in her path, she knew immediately.

"Evenin' Miss," the stranger said in his scratchy voice. "What do we got in that little purse of ours, 'eh?"

"Leave me alone," Alice said shyly. She wanted to get back to her apartment, wanted to get through her mourning. She felt not fear, but annoyance at any obstacle to her reaching her intended destination.

"C'mon, girlie," the thug said. "Hand it over or I'll have to work you over for it."

Alice turned to reverse her course, head back to the main avenue where it was brighter, more populated, and safer. As she turned, she felt a strong, large hand grasp her arm and begin the motion of spinning her roughly around. She was turned and found herself face to face with the ugly stranger. She could smell the stench of poor hygiene and cheap booze on his hot breath and feel the coarse calluses on his fingers as they tightened on her slim wrist. The mugger pulled her closer to him, seemingly intent on rape in addition to robbery.

Alice did not scream. She made no sound at first. She closed her eyes for the briefest of instants and saw a different life flash before her inner vision. She saw a life of desperation and violence that she thought she had left behind forever, buried like the past often should be. A feeling of forceful confidence, almost cockiness came over Alice. Her entire expression changed. She became someone she had once been and had never expected to be again.

"Getcher filthy hands offa me ya dirty animal!" Alice Carter suddenly roared out in a voice different from one that Julia Carter or Tommy or Larry Epstein had ever heard. It was the rough Cockney of the nastier parts of London and it came with fury and swift action.

Alice wrenched her arm free of her attacker's grip. Her hand free, she formed her soft fingers into a fist and swung, full force, at his face. She could feel his whiskers scrape her skin as her knuckles landed against his bulbous nose. The cracking sound was audible as the nose broke and blood splashed forth from both his nostrils at once. He let out a choked groan which turned into a sharp soprano shriek as Alice brought her knee up, with no lack of anger behind it, into his crotch. He fell upon the dirty concrete of the alley and curled up into a whimpering ball of pain and helplessness. As Alice turned to walk away from the victimizer who had become the victim, she resisted the urge to completely devolve into a previous version of herself and spit on him. She could smell the sharp stench of urine as she walked away; the pain had made the ruffian lose control of his bladder.

❋ ❋ ❋

Alice woke up the next morning as the sunlight came in through the apartment window. She was on her familiar bed, but alone there for the first time since she had married Tommy. She was still in the clothes she had worn when she had walked there. Her hand throbbed and she looked down at it to see that she had split the flesh on one knuckle. As she looked at the now clotted wound, she remembered what had happened in the alley the night before. She remembered who she had become again, if only for those few brief seconds of violence and self-preservation. The thought of that temporary transformation made scenes from her childhood flood into her mind. She welcomed the avalanche of memories as a welcome respite from the thoughts of Tommy and his being gone that had haunted her for the last three days. She let the memories wash over her; some were good, some were bad, but they were, at least, of a time when she knew less pain than had been thrust at her with Tommy's passing.

"Getcher filthy hands offa me ya dirty animal!"

She saw the place she had called Home when she had been a little girl. She had never known her mother, a victim of a fever she had contracted shortly after giving birth to Alice. But her father she would never forget. Life with Daddy had been happy, joyous, and so full of love that Alice had never really felt the lack of a mother in her life. Her father earned enough from the local mill, supplemented by his Army pension, to afford a decent little cottage for him and his little girl. Village life was good, carefree as much as any life could be, and peaceful. Alice would go to school and then rush home and wait for her father. They would eat supper and then he would tell her stories of his youth, of what it was like growing up in that same little village over forty years earlier.

On Sundays, when there was no work and no school, and after morning church services, Alice and her father would make their pilgrimages into the woods. Out there, alone among the trees, Daddy would stand empty beer bottles upon old tree stumps and he would teach Alice how to shoot a pistol. She became quite a good shot for a little girl. It was an odd thing for a father to teach a daughter, but it was what Alice's father knew and so he felt the need to pass it on to his child, regardless of whether or not it might be considered proper by those who made it their business to tell other people what was, or was not, proper.

Alice's father had been a sergeant major before retiring and taking a job at the mill and raising his daughter in the same village where he had grown up years before. As much as his skill with a pistol amazed her, she was aware that he had been an even more expert marksman in his army days. By the time Alice had been born, he had taught himself to shoot left-handed after leaving his right arm in a trench in France during The Great War.

Those fond times in that little village were not destined to last forever and Alice would know some sorrow before she had left her childhood. When she was fifteen, her father's heart gave out when he overexerted himself at the mill. He had always prided himself on the ability to do just as much work as those men who still had both arms to make a living with. One day, he just pushed himself too hard and that was it for him; Alice was an orphan.

She knew that if she stayed there, in the place she had grown up in, having no living relatives, she'd be sent to an orphanage, watched and controlled by rules and regulations every moment of every day and every night. She could not bear the idea of that state of captivity and so she decided to take her chances with fending for herself in the world beyond the boundaries of that little town. Before the orphan collectors came for her, she had gathered up what little money and valuables were in that little cottage and she had slipped away to try to make her way to London, where nobody knew her and nobody would try to interfere with her precious freedom.

She found London, but had no idea how quickly her little stash of money would run dry. She turned sixteen homeless and cold and hungry and alone. She wouldn't sell herself to survive; she couldn't bring herself to do such a dreadful thing, so she stole. That was bad and she felt a great guilt in her gut every time she took a bite from some purloined loaf or snatched apple, but it kept her alive without having to resort to an even greater sin.

On those East End streets, she learned to do other things to keep herself alive. There were always those who would try to steal what little she had, including her innocence, so she learned to quickly, efficiently, and decisively either escape from those who posed a threat, or viciously remind them that she was not one to be taken advantage of so easily. She learned to use her fists, her nails, her teeth when she had to.

For nearly three years, Alice had lived like a rat. She scraped together food, worked what small, menial jobs she could find, and just barely managed to stay alive. When she could stand that wretched existence no longer, she decided to take a chance at finding something else or, at least, something new. She used her street skills, her knack for hiding and evading detection, and her ability to survive on the crumbs and leftovers of others to stow away on a passenger ship bound for New York. She thought she would die sooner or later, probably starving or freezing to death in some slum alley, so she decided that America was as good a place as England to end up dead; at least she'd see a new land before it was all over, she convinced herself.

As the ship sailed into New York Harbor and Alice gazed out through the porthole of the empty cabin she had hidden in, the sun rising over the vast and proud city, she felt her heart come aglow with wonder and she vowed that she would survive there in that Promised Land, making a fresh start and leaving behind the life of just barely scraping by that had gotten her through since her father's death.

Once in Manhattan, she engaged in one last use of her thieving skills, taking just enough money from a shopkeeper who looked away from his cashbox for too long, just enough to buy a decent set of clothes and rent a small room for a few weeks. She even returned the money, dropping it in the shop's doorway a few minutes before she knew the owner would be opening up for the day, once she had made enough on her own to repay the unwilling loan. Once she had the clothes to look presentable, she had found a job. It wasn't anything spectacular, just a position in a factory that made handbags, but it was respectable enough and for the first time in her life on her own, Alice had felt human again.

She worked hard at the factory, saving some pennies when she could and working on shedding her accent and speaking like a real American girl and blending in with her adopted surroundings. One evening after a long day's work, she was asked to go to a local college football game by Joanie Watkins, a friend from the factory. She accepted and soon found herself sitting in the bleachers watching a game she didn't understand at all. She was quite bored until her eyes happened to fall on the sight of the quarterback, of the winning team, taking off his helmet after the final play of the game. It was then, at the moment she first caught sight of Tommy Carter, that her life had changed forever. He was tall, broad-shouldered, blond and blue-eyed. To Alice, Tommy Carter was America. Once she had seen him, she knew she had to have him.

Two years later, the two were married. She never told him about her adolescence on the streets of London's East End. She never told him how she had stolen and sneaked and scraped for dear life. Tommy knew that his young bride had been born in England, but he knew little else of her life before she had sailed to America. He loved her, and she loved him, and nothing else mattered.

Tommy had always wanted to be a detective. He graduated the Police Academy and started his term of duty as a patrolman, hoping to make the Detective's Bureau before too much time went by. Alice would never forget how handsome he had looked the first time she had seen him in his brand new uniform, strong chest decorated with shiny buttons and a brilliant, brand new badge. She watched him clean his revolver and shine his shoes and hang his uniform hat on the hook by the door of their little apartment and then Officer Carter, her husband, her beloved, celebrated his graduation and his new place on the city's police force by making love to his wife.

Alice's heart swelled with love and pride as she watched him leave in the morning to go and walk his beat. He left the same way every morning for the next two years: with a kiss and a smile and a little twirl of his nightstick. Every day for those two wonderful years, Alice Carter watched her husband, her Tommy, her Mister America head out into the streets to guard the innocent, bring the guilty to justice, and always do what was right. And then, one dark evening, he was gone forever.

❀ ❀ ❀

The funeral day arrived. Alice walked to the gravesite with Tommy's mother beside her and Larry Epstein, who had been Tommy's closest friend on the force, on the other side. She looked through her black veil; the scene was blurred by her tear-filled eyes and she barely heard a word the minister said. By the time it was over and the police band's bagpipes had blasted out their final wail, Alice was exhausted. Larry drove her and her mother-in-law back to Julia's house and Alice sat in Tommy's old room wondering what she could do now, a widow at twenty-three, with just an elderly mother-in-law and no formal education.

Months passed by. Alice's meager saving ran out and she had to give up the apartment. She moved in with Julia. The older lady was happy to have company, but Alice felt like a freeloader, a parasite. Every day she would check the newspaper, hoping and praying that someone had been arrested or questioned or that some progress had been made in the investigation of Tommy's death, but no such article appeared. Day after day, week after week, month after month: nothing.

A year to the day after the darkest day of her life, Alice picked up the telephone in Julia's kitchen and called the police department. When the desk sergeant answered, she asked for Officer Epstein.

"Oh...you mean Detective Epstein, do you Miss?" said the Irish-brogue on the other end of the line. "The lad got himself promoted just the other day, sure enough he did! Please stay on the line and I'll connect you to his office."

An hour later, in a small corner diner a few blocks from the house where Alice had been staying with her mother-in-law, the bell above the door jingled as a trench-coated man walked in and made his way over to the booth where Alice was already seated, slowly sipping a cup of coffee that had been too hot to drink when it had first been delivered by the waitress five minutes earlier.

Detective Larry Epstein took off his fedora, unbuttoned his coat, sat down across from Alice, and lit a cigarette. He offered one to Alice but she shook her head, having never taken up smoking.

"How are you doing, Alice?" Epstein asked after his first long drag.

"I'm managing, Larry. Thanks," Alice said between sips of coffee. "I'm doing all right, I suppose. Julia's all right too; she's got a lot of energy for a lady her age. I don't know what I'd do without her. I've been looking for a new job; I don't want to go back to the factory work I did before...before I married Tommy. Congratulations on the promotion, by the way."

Epstein finished his cigarette and snuffed it out in the table's ashtray just as the waitress brought his coffee over and refilled Alice's cup. "Thanks, Alice, and I'm glad to hear you're doing well enough...but I don't think you called the precinct just to get me to come and drink coffee and catch up. What's on your mind?"

Alice's pleasant, conversational face shifted into a concerned, almost angry look. She was clearly frustrated. Even if Larry Epstein had not been a detective, he still would have noticed the distress on the young widow's face.

"Damn it, Larry," Alice blurted out, unconcerned about her swearing being perceived as unladylike. "It's been a year, it's a year today since Tommy died...and nothing's been done about it. There's been nothing in the papers, they haven't arrested anyone. Does anybody in the police department have any idea at all what happened that day? Larry, I just want to know why Tommy isn't here with me anymore. Is that too much to ask? Please, Larry, just tell me you have some news; any news at all!"

Epstein closed his eyes for a moment, fighting back the nervousness that was written on his face. It was obvious to Alice that she was not going to like what the detective was going to say next. Epstein took out another cigarette and lit it before speaking again.

"Alice, I'm sorry. I didn't want to have to be the one to tell you this but...they've closed the case. The investigation of Tom's death is not going to go any further."

Alice slammed her coffee cup down on the table; the hot liquid spilled over the rim of the cup and dribbled onto the table. "What? What do you mean they closed the case? Tommy was a cop, Larry, and he was gunned down in that empty apartment! I'm no cop myself...but I know the police just don't close a case and forget about it when one of their own is murdered! What the hell is going on, Larry! Damn it! I have a right to know; I was his wife!"

Detective Epstein stood up and began to button his trench coat. He grabbed his hat and backed away from the table. "I can't stay here, Alice. I can't talk about this anymore. I have to go now."

The young detective walked out of the diner without saying another word. Alice drank the little bit of coffee that was left in her cup and went home, back to Julia Carter's house. She sat in her room, the room that Tommy had grown up in. She sat alone through the remaining hours of the day and thought of Tommy and how much she needed to know why he had been killed and wondered how she could ever find out if she didn't even have Tommy's best friend to help her. It had been a year since she had lost Tommy; she thought she was getting over it, getting her head screwed back on straight. She had been wrong. She sat on the edge of the bed and cried. She didn't come out of that room until the next morning.

❀ ❀ ❀

A week later, after considering her options, Alice dressed in her best daytime outfit. She donned a new blouse, got into her skirt, pulled on her stockings and her best pair of shoes and made her way down to the police station where Tommy had been posted. She ignored the door to the detectives' offices, having no desire to speak to Larry Epstein after he had so abruptly left her sitting in the diner.

She made her way to the topmost floor of the precinct house and demanded to see the man in charge. Ten minutes later she was let into the office of Captain Edward Stern. Stern was a career cop, in his fifties, balding and large, but not obese by any means. Alice walked into his office and found him sitting behind his desk filling his pipe with tobacco.

"Good morning, Miss," the captain said, looking up from his pipe and not hiding the fact that he had taken notice of her skirt and the lithe pair of legs that it only partially hid from his admiring view. "The desk sergeant said you had demanded to see me. What can be so important that you'd have to barge in here and see the captain and not one of my men?"

"Captain Stern, I'm sure you don't remember me. We only met a few times. My name is Alice Carter."

Stern stood up, ignored his pipe, and smiled. "Mrs. Carter; you're Officer Carter's wife. I'm so sorry I didn't recognize you. How are you? I suppose I haven't seen you since poor Tom's funeral. What brings you here this morning? Can I offer you anything? I can have some coffee brought in, or something stronger if you prefer." He gestured at the liquor cabinet behind his desk.

"Nothing, Captain, but thank you," Alice said. "Actually, sir, I have a bit of a problem. You see, the money that Tommy and I saved is nearly run dry and I can't seem to find a job. Tommy always spoke highly of you, Captain, and I thought maybe you could help me. I just need to find some work. I was wondering if the police department had any openings for secretaries."

Captain Stern looked Alice up and down again. He obviously liked what he saw and Alice decided to take advantage of the captain's admiration. She smiled sweetly and waited for him to answer.

"Can you type well?" Stern asked.

"Yes I can, sir," Alice lied. She had rarely had reason to type up to that point in her life, but she was desperate to find a way inside that police precinct so she told the captain what he wanted to hear.

"Well then, Mrs. Carter; can I call you Alice, dear? I have been thinking of adding another person to my staff. I seem to keep falling behind on my paperwork; you have no idea how busy a police captain can be. I suppose I could hire you on a trial basis, see exactly what you're capable of. Why don't you come back on Monday, eight o'clock sharp? We'll see how it all works out."

Alice repeated the smile she had flashed the first time. "Thank you, Captain. I promise I won't disappoint you." She left the office, walking slowly to make certain that Stern had time to admire the view as she departed. She felt a bit dirty using her looks to get what she wanted, but when she thought of Tommy and how desperately she wanted answers, the guilt flew out of her mind.

As she walked home after the interview with Stern, she wondered what she had gotten herself into. She had to report for work on Monday morning. It was Thursday. That gave her four days to make a good secretary of herself. She quickened her walking pace; she knew what she had to do.

Alice went straight back to Julia Carter's house. She made her way up to the attic. Several weeks earlier, she had gone up to that storage space to retrieve something for her mother-in-law, who had grown too old to climb ladders anymore. While up in that attic, she had noticed an old typewriter. Now she went up into that room again and carried the typewriter down to the second floor of the house. She placed it on the desk in the room she had been using and inserted some paper. She tried to type, but it was clumsy, awkward, and slow. She grew frustrated quickly. Trying to think of a way to make the practicing less torturous, she realized that having something to write about might make it easier. She put in a fresh sheet of paper and thought of Tommy. "Dearest Tommy," she began to type, "I've missed you terribly and I so very much want to tell you everything that's been happening since you went away. I hope that somehow, wherever you are, you might be able to see this letter and know that I'm thinking of you, as I always will be..."

Alice typed for hours and hours, pouring her heart and her words into a long letter that would never be read. She focused on Tommy and everything she wanted to say to him, all the feelings she wished she could express to him in person, but never could now that he was gone. It no longer felt like difficult practice, for it now had a purpose behind it. She typed and typed, the order of the keys becoming etched into her mind as she pounded the letters onto the page, then the next page, and then a dozen more after that. She typed faster, more confidently, the ease of the task increasing as she grew more proficient. She typed that day and the next and the day after that. By Sunday evening, having barely taken the time to eat or rest since Thursday, much to the concern of her mother-in-law, Alice had transformed herself into a typist of considerable skill and speed.

❖ ❖ ❖

Monday morning came and Alice arrived at the police station at quarter to eight. She made her way upstairs and was seated behind the secondary desk inside Captain Stern's office by the time the precinct chief had arrived. The first morning went by quickly enough. Captain Stern dictated some reports to Alice and she used her newfound typing ability; it did not let her down. Stern seemed like he would be a decent enough man to work for, although his long looks in her direction often felt like more than casual glances and Alice did feel a bit uncomfortable at times. Even so, her true reasons for taking the secretary's job at the precinct were always on her mind and that made the slight awkwardness of being in the room with Stern all day a bit more bearable.

At times, Alice would be asked to bring papers or other items to the various parts of the station. She looked forward to those occasions. It gave her a few minutes away from Captain Stern, but more importantly it gave her a chance to familiarize herself with the layout of the building, something she would have to be aware of when the right time came for her to do what she really wanted to do in that precinct building.

The weeks rolled by and the job went well. Captain Stern no longer made her nervous; she came to realize that he was just a lonely cop who had been so engrossed by his career that he'd never bothered to settle down and marry. Casting a lustful glance in the direction of a pretty young woman was no reason to condemn the captain, Alice decided. She actually enjoyed the work, even if her true purpose was something other than the acquisition of the small paycheck she brought home each week.

She tried to avoid Detective Epstein as much as possible. She hadn't forgiven him for what he had said, or not said, at the diner. If she saw him in the halls or offices, she would say "Hello" or nod, but she made no attempt to engage him in conversation. He seemed to be steering clear of her as well. Perhaps, Alice suspected, Larry Epstein knew more than he had told her over that coffee, perhaps she would someday learn what had upset him so when she had begged for information on the progress of the case of Tommy's death.

Two months after beginning work at the police precinct, Alice decided she had learned the layout of the building and the daily routine of police business thoroughly enough that she could proceed with what she had in mind as her next step toward discovering the truth about Tommy's death.

"I'm heading home for the night, Alice," said Captain Stern after a loud yawn. "Have a good night, my dear."

"If you don't mind, sir," Alice answered, "I'd like to stay here and use the office for a while longer. Your paperwork has been falling into disarray and I thought I'd do some organizing, if it's all right with you, sir."

"You never cease to amaze me, young lady," Stern said. "I wish half the real cops here were as motivated as you are. Suit yourself then, Alice, but I'm quitting now."

Alice moved papers around, typed a bit, pretended to be doing something productive as the dusk came and went and night fell in fullness over New York City. When it was fully dark outside and Alice could hear the noise in the hallways outside the captain's office lessening, she knew that the emptier hours in that building had begun.

The precinct was never completely unoccupied. The first floor always had its share of people moving about. There was always a desk sergeant on duty and patrolmen coming in and out. The two upper floors were much less busy in the night hours than during the day. The top floor, where she worked, was left empty overnight once the captain and his immediate staff had gone home for the night. The floor below hers, the second floor, housed the detectives' department and the large filing room where all the closed case reports were left in storage. Alice knew, from her two months of memorizing the routine of the department, that there was usually just one lone detective present from ten o'clock until about six in the morning. Other plainclothesmen were on duty overnight, but they rarely stayed in the offices, seeing no need to stay glued to their desks when the captain was home sleeping and not around to keep them in line.

That near-emptiness of the two upper floors was the reason why Alice had chosen to stay late that night. She wanted to get into the records room and see if she could find the file on Tommy's murder. Having only one detective to avoid being seen by made things a lot easier than they would have been in the impossible daylight hours when the place was abuzz with activities of all kinds. As a mere secretary and civilian, Alice was forbidden from accessing the sealed records unless accompanied by an authorized officer. She had no intention of asking Captain Stern for permission to read the file on Tommy's death, for she suspected, based on the early closure of the case and on Epstein's reaction to her questions months earlier, that there was something very strange about the case, something the department was trying to hide.

When she was certain that the third floor was empty except for her, Alice put aside the papers she had been fiddling with. She got up from her desk and glanced around, a last assurance to herself that she was alone. She put her mind into focus, gathering the instincts she had developed as a younger woman when she had survived by sneaking around the streets of the East End and drawing as little attention to herself as possible. Like the old cliché says about riding a bicycle, certain skills are never lost, no matter how much one might expect them to be eroded by time.

Alice kicked off her shoes to minimize the sound of her walking around the building. While there might have been fewer people around to catch sight of her, the emptiness could also be a disadvantage as the lack of noise would make any sound seem magnified to anyone close enough to hear it. The clicking of heels on the hard floors would give her away for sure had she not taken that precaution.

She slipped out the door of Captain Stern's office and into the hallway. Slowly, carefully, silently, she crept along the corridor and made her way to the staircase. Through the next door and onto the steps she went, the only sound the slight whisper of the fabric of her skirt as she moved gracefully and clandestinely along.

She tiptoed down the stairs to the door that led from the stairwell out into the second-story halls. She opened the door slowly, poking her head out to glance around. No one was in sight. She went out into the hallway. About a hundred feet ahead would be two rooms, the only rooms on that floor that mattered to her on that night. She moved on. The detectives' offices were on her left. Through the windows of the offices she could see about a dozen empty desks. Only one lamp was lit, illuminating a stack of paperwork that sat upon the desk in front of the lone detective in the building. The coffee mug next to the paperwork let loose no steam so Alice assumed it had gone cold. The slumped posture of the man in the accompanying chair showed her that the detective, whom she did not recognize from her view of the back of his head, had dozed off, the victim of too much paperwork and the boredom that went along with it.

She breathed a short breath of relief at the sight of the dozing detective. The man's slumber would make her job easier. On her right was the entrance to the records room. She put a hand to her breast, taking a key from within her bra. She had taken the key from the drawer where she had known that Captain Stern kept it. She had hidden it in her bra as a precaution. Had she been caught in the act of sneaking around the halls, that spot would be the last place a male police officer would have dared to look unless he was absolutely certain that Alice was up to no good. Hiding the key there would have given her extra time to figure out a way to get rid of it had she been caught.

She slipped the key into the lock and turned the doorknob. It opened. She slipped inside the dark records room and shut the door behind her. There were several lamps in the room, but she lit only one; the less light there was, the less chance there would be of it being seen under the door. She slipped the key back into her blouse and looked at the rows of filing cabinets that lined the walls. She knew that murder cases were filed under the last name of the victim. She walked over to the drawer marked with a "C."

Caldwell, Campbell, Candini; she rifled through the files in their thick folders. Murder files were always thick, she knew from handling the files on open cases as they crossed her desk on their way to the captain. Murder was taken seriously, as it should have been, and those files contained every report, every note, every statement the detectives had reason to write out in the course of an investigation.

Carter! There it was, she thought. No, wait. There were several Carters. Andrew Carter, Joan Carter, Miles Carter, Thomas Carter! There it was. Alice's slender fingers gripped the top of the folder and pulled it from its place in the drawer. She gasped in shock when she saw the slimness of the file. She placed it in direct light of the single lit lamp and opened it. Nothing! There was almost nothing inside it. Alice looked at the single sheet of paper in the folder; it was just the initial report of the crime: address and time of incident; name, age, and occupation of the victim; and the first notes, amounting to nothing substantial, of the detective who had been first on the scene, one Detective First Class Douglas Brown.

Alice's mind spun with confusion. She had known that there had not been much of an investigation; it had been called off far too quickly for it to have gone too far, but this was nothing. As if there had been no investigation at all, the file was nearly empty. She looked that single sheet of paper over one last time. On the bottom was a notation: "Case closed by order of…"

"By order of who?" Alice whispered to herself, just barely keeping calm enough to not scream the question out loud. The name at the end of the sentence had been blacked out, covered in ink. Who had closed the case? She held the paper up in front of the lamplight, trying to squint through the ink, praying that her eyes could penetrate the black blotch of camouflage, but it was no use. Alice cursed under her breath. She repeated the name Douglas Brown to herself several times, etching it into her memory; that detective's name was the only lead she had and she vowed to find Brown and learn whatever he knew. The name didn't ring a bell in her mind, so she assumed he was no longer assigned to that precinct. If he was, she would have known his name from whatever case files he was currently working on. "Douglas Brown," she repeated.

She shoved the folder with her dead husband's name on it back into the drawer, closed the cabinet, and snuck back out into the hall. Within minutes she was back up on the third floor, gathering her things and leaving the building. She'd take the open route out now; there was no need for anymore sneaking around. She left by the front floor on the first floor, smiling and giving a wave to the sergeant on duty as she left.

❄ ❄ ❄

Alice got no sleep that night. She tossed and turned and thought and grew angrier and angrier. It made no sense to her. Tommy had been a cop, a member of the fraternity that the police department was supposed to be. They were supposed to look out for their own. When one of them was killed, the others were supposed to spare no expense, make no excuses, stop at nothing to find whoever was responsible and bring him to justice. Why hadn't that been done for Tommy? Why had only the barest formality of an investigation been attempted? Who had given the order to close the case so quickly…and why was his name blacked out on that report?

Alice's head spun round and round as her grief, the sadness she had buried and convinced herself was gone, came rising back up to the surface of her consciousness. She sat up in bed, sweat soaking her nightgown, her hands trembling, and the moonlight that shone in the window reflecting in her luminous, tear-filled blue eyes.

"Justice," Alice Carter said out loud. She got out of bed and went to the closet. She ripped open the closet door and stood staring at the pile of boxes, all which remained of the contents of the apartment she had once shared with the man of her dreams, the man that America had given her, the man she loved more than any other, her husband.

She found the box she was looking for. She pulled it out and tore off the lid. She reached in and took out a large, folded white garment. She went to another box, pulling out a small metal object. She placed both objects into a bag that she had lying in the room. Her mind spun with ideas, she knew what she had to do next, but some of it would have to wait until morning. She knew she would not sleep; her heart raced too fast, her nerves shook, her head ached. She sat down on the floor and gazed out the window at the moon.

When morning arrived, Alice left early, ignoring the breakfast that Julia had made, and headed to the nearest collection of shops. It was Sunday; no work at the police station for her. She shopped quickly and determinedly, acquiring the few items that had occurred to her the night before. She bought two bottles of dye, one red and one black. She purchased a pair of metal shears, strong scissors capable of cutting through thin sheets of many metallic materials. She went to the Army Surplus store

*She placed the file in the direct light of the single lit lamp and opened it. Nothing!
There was almost nothing inside it.*

and bought a pair of thick leather gloves and a pair of heavy combat boots, hard to find in a size that fit her as they were not made for women, but there were small soldiers after all and she eventually found a pair. Her last stop was a pawn shop. It was not the sort of place a proper young woman would go, but she had no concerns about being proper at that moment. She had one thing on her mind, and it would be found in a place like that. When she left the pawn shop, she shoved the pistol all the way down to the bottom of her bag, making certain that no one should see it if they happened to glance at what she was carrying.

She tried to spend the rest of the day as normally as possible. She had lunch with Julia, listened to the afternoon radio programs, helped Julia in the garden for awhile, ate supper, and retired to her room at a fairly early hour, wanting to do nothing that might indicate to Julia that she was up to anything unusual. If her mother-in-law found out what she was planning, Alice knew, the elderly woman would have her committed.

She sat on her bed and waited for an hour after she had gone upstairs. She wanted to be sure that Julia had gone to sleep so that there would be no unwelcome interruptions to her night's work. When she was certain that no one would bother her, she began. She took out two buckets she had brought up after working in the garden earlier that day. She took out the white garment she had pulled from the closet the night before. She tore a strip from part of the garment. She stuffed the larger piece of the garment into one of the buckets. Into that bucket she poured the black dye she had bought that morning. The smaller piece of material that she had torn from the larger piece, she put into the second bucket. Onto that, she poured the entire bottle of red dye. She took the boots and gloves she had bought from her shopping bag and laid them on the floor. She took the gun and placed it beside them. Finally, she took out the small metal object she had found in her closet the night before and held it up in front of her tearful eyes. It glinted in the dim light of her room at night. She held it there in front of her face for a long time: the badge that had once adorned the uniform of Officer Thomas Carter. She breathed deeply to prepare herself for what she was about to do. She put the badge to her lips and gently kissed it. Then she took out her new metal shears and cut the badge into pieces.

When she was finished, Alice took all of those things and put them into the closet, leaving the cloth in the buckets to soak up all the dye. She closed the closet door and climbed into bed. She fell asleep and dreamed of all the parts of her life. As she slept, the past swirled around in her head like wet cement in a mixer truck. Who was she? Who was Alice? She kept asking herself that question as she slept and dreamed. Was she the innocent little girl who took infinite joy in watching the bullets she fired shatter those old glass beer bottles in the English countryside? Was she the teenager, in rags and starving and scraping by and fighting in the streets to escape the would-be rapists in the night on the East End? Was she the pretty young woman, trying so hard to act and talk like an American girl and wishing more than anything that the handsome young college football star would notice the way she looked at him? Was she the proud young wife, so in love with the handsome policeman who came home to her every night? Or was she the poor sorrowful widow, robbed of her husband in a single instant of terrible violence? Who was Alice Carter? Who had she been in the past…and who would she be when the sun rose again? Who would she be the next time night fell on New York City?

❈ ❈ ❈

Alice reported to work at Captain Stern's office the next morning. She spent the first two hours taking dictation and waiting for the opportunity to do what she had to do next. The chance finally came when Captain Stern went downstairs to speak to the patrolmen about some new name on the city's Most Wanted list.

Alice had already determined that Detective Douglas Brown was no longer assigned to her precinct. Now she needed to find out either where he was now posted or where he lived. It was not unusual for her to make calls to the main police records bureau on order of Captain Stern. She made such a call then, but without Stern's authorization. It didn't matter, she knew, as the person she was speaking to over the phone had no way of knowing that Stern had not requested the information. As long as Stern didn't know about the call, Alice would be fine. Within minutes, she had information on Detective First Class Brown. He had not been transferred, but had taken an early retirement. He still lived in the city and the secretary at the main records office had been all too happy to supply Alice with Brown's home address, especially since it was, Alice had told her, for the purpose of planning a surprise party for Brown's birthday. Had the poor woman known why Alice really wanted the address, she would have shouted out for every policeman within earshot.

The rest of the day was uneventful. Alice went home at the usual time, dined with Julia, talked with her for awhile as they both enjoyed a glass of wine, and finally went to her room. She did not, however, go to bed. Alice's night was just beginning.

❈ ❈ ❈

No one, had they been watching the house, would have even noticed Alice leaving, so well had her life on the London streets taught her to sneak through the shadows. It was no difficult task for her to climb out the second-story window, maneuver her way down the exterior wall by clinging to the drainpipe, and run quietly through the backyard and into the alleys that ran between pieces of property in that residential neighborhood. She was impressed by how little extraneous sound her new boots made if one tread carefully, but still quickly, while wearing them.

She could not afford to be seen by anyone, strangely attired as she now was. The place where she was going was several miles away, too far to walk and a cab was out of the question. Still, Alice was resourceful and she quickly came up with a solution. She spotted a truck heading in the general direction of her destination. She ran through the shadows, keeping the vehicle in sight. When it stopped to let another car turn onto the street, she pounced, grabbing onto the rear door of the truck and climbing up, hitching a ride, invisible to the driver and so darkly clad that even pedestrians would have had to be looking for her to have spotted her. When the truck started to go off the path she needed to follow, Alice would jump off and catch another passing truck. As she moved from ride to ride, getting ever closer to where she wanted to be, she was pleasantly surprised, satisfied, at how well that method of travel seemed to be working for her.

Thirty minutes later, Douglas Brown sat up in bed. He rubbed the sleep from his eyes and shoved aside the lock of his thick gray hair that tickled his forehead. He looked around quickly, squinting at the shadows. He had thought he had heard a sound and it was not unknown for burglaries to take place in the area where his apartment was situated, so he had come out of sleep in a state of some alarm. He saw no movement in his room, heard no further noise, so he started to lean back against his pillow, ready to resume his rest.

"You will not go back to sleep so soon."

"What? Who said that? Who's there?" Brown shouted at the shadows. "Come out where I can see you! Are you a girl? You sound like a girl! Girls don't grow up to be prowlers! Come out of the dark and I'll give you a good spanking!"

Brown's taunting tirade ended abruptly when something came out of the shadows and stood in the pale light of the streetlamps that shone through the window. Brown fell silent, felt his insides quiver like pudding as he took in the sight of what stood before him.

It was shaped like a woman, but adorned like something out of a nightmare inspired by Hell itself. It was dressed all in black from its feet up to its neck. The strange garment it wore looked, for all that Douglas Brown could see, like a wedding dress, except that it was black as coal and torn short at the level of the ankles. Over the surreal parody of a bridal gown was a black cloak that stretched out like the wings of a bat or of some awful raven from Poe's absinthe-induced rhyming rants. The creature's hands were concealed within the folds of its terrible costume so that Brown could not tell if it wielded a weapon of any kind. The consistent, all-consuming blackness of its attire was broken only when the observer's gaze looked upon the head, for the color changed there. The shape of the head was feminine enough and Brown could see long dark hair flowing and cascading down around the shoulders. The face, however, was unseen, hidden behind a piece of crimson lace that fluttered slightly as it was touched by the breeze that came in through the open window. That striking, blood-colored, ethereal and darkly lovely red veil sent a strange sensation of absolute horror shooting through every inch of Douglas Brown's body and soul. What strange apparition stood before him? What was it…and what did it want? The retired detective did not know what to do, did not know what to say.

The apparition spoke again before Brown could utter another word. The voice was female; of that Brown was sure, but it was unlike any other voice he had ever heard. The accent was odd, like an American woman with a voice that seemed to be fighting back a long-buried British tint. It was also somehow inhuman, as if the pitch and volume were fluctuating as the emotions behind the words rose and fell like waves upon a stormy sea. It was an eerie, almost supernatural sound, and Brown was not sure if he were awake and really seeing and hearing the strange woman-shaped creature, or if he was trapped in some strange surreal nightmare from which waking would not happen fast enough to quell his fear.

"Douglas Brown," the voice called out to him. "This is not a dream. I am real... and you are right to be afraid. I am a ghost of grief and a spirit of sorrow, an angel of anguish and a demon of despair. I am the Red Veil! I am the shroud over the face of every mourner; I am vengeance in the form of a woman! My body is the color of death and my face is the shade of blood."

Brown could feel his heart pounding in his chest as he hoped he was experiencing some strange, sickness-induced hallucination, but feared that it was some grim, gruesome reality staring at him as he lay vulnerable in his bed in the middle of the night. "What do you want?" he murmured nervously, wanting to pull the blankets over his head and hide from the terrible sight until his mother came to comfort him and assure him that it was only a dream. Twenty years on the police force of the biggest city in the world and Douglas Brown had been reduced to nothing more than a forty-five year old child, quivering in the dark.

"I want answers," wailed the Red Veil. "I will ask questions...and you, Douglas Brown, shall answer them. You will tell me the truth...or you will pay the price for your dishonesty, for my patience is short...and my claws are sharp!"

As the strange being before Douglas Brown's eyes spoke those words, that horrible threat of pain and violence, it drew forth from under its cloak its right hand and held that hand in the light where Brown could see it. The hand was gloved, clad in black like the rest of the nightmare being. Upon the ends of its fingers were sharp pointed things, talons that gleamed as the light of the lamps outside reflected off of the steel-like material that composed those dreadful nails. Brown gasped, truly suspecting, in his fear-induced stupor, that the thing that stood before him was not human, no flesh and blood woman, but a she-demon from the bowels of Hell. Had he been able to look more closely at those claws, those terrible knife-like things that flashed in the dim light as the beast flexed its fingers, Brown might have realized that they were the shards of a police badge that had been cut into strips, jagged edges unsmoothed and deadly should they make contact with anything as flimsy and fragile as human flesh.

"What...what do you want to know?" Brown could barely make the words rise into his throat and fly from his trembling lips.

"One year ago," said the Red Veil, "there was a death, a murder. Bullets destroyed a young man, a policeman, Officer Thomas Michael Carter. You went to the scene, you wrote a report, and that was all that you did. The case was terminated shortly thereafter, never solved, taken no further. Why, Douglas Brown? Why did it end so soon? Someone told you to stop the investigation! That much I know! You retired early and here you sit in your bed, wasting years that could have been spent still bringing killers to justice and protecting the innocent and avenging brave slain souls like Thomas Carter. Were you told to retire, Douglas Brown? Was the man who halted the investigation the same man who told you to leave the force? Did he give you an early pension in return for your silence, your secrecy, your loyalty to some dreadful conspiracy that leaves poor young Officer Carter unavenged? Is that what happened, Brown? Is it?"

"I…I don't know much," Brown stammered. "I was the first one to go when we got the call about shots that night. I found Officer Carter in that little apartment. He was already dead when I got there. It only took a couple of days for them to tell me to give up the case. It turned out to be my last case. I don't know why they told me to quit; I really don't. I swear that's all I know about the whole thing. It was a shame about Carter. He was a good cop; he had potential, might have been a detective one day. But I don't know who shot him. I don't know why the case was closed."

The voice from the veiled face was silent for moments that seemed, to Brown, to go on for hours. The face was completely concealed, but a tilt of the head gave the impression that it was deep in thought, weighing the options of what to say or do next. Brown prayed that he would not soon feel the bite of those terrible talons that adorned the fingers of that black-gloved hand.

"I believe you," said the Red Veil, and Douglas Brown's heart slowed down at least enough so that it no longer felt ready to explode forth from his chest. "You don't know who the killer was. But you do know who told you to stop the investigation and retire. Speak his name now, Douglas Brown, and you will still live when the sun rises in the morning."

She flashed the claws again, tapping them against each other like vampiric castanets.

"Falk; Captain Samuel Falk," Brown responded to the implied threat of the clinking claws.

"Falk," the Red Veil repeated Brown's words. "I will leave you now, Douglas Brown. Do not rise from that bed until the first rays of dawn penetrate your window."

There was a blur of movement; the strange creature with which he had just conversed seemed to melt into the shadows and fade from existence, and Douglas Brown was alone. He did not leave his bed that night.

※ ※ ※

Alice Carter reported to work as usual the next morning. She was tired, but remedied that with an extra coffee as soon as she arrived at the stationhouse. The morning was uneventful and she waited for the right time to utilize the ploy she had devised to get the piece of information she wanted next to help her in the quest that was the real reason she had taken the job as Captain Stern's secretary.

Stern had just returned from his lunch break. It had been vital to Alice's plan that he would leave his office for a brief time.

"Captain," she said, "I'm afraid I made a bit of a mistake. While you were out, another precinct called. They asked me to send a file over to their address, but I seem to have forgotten which precinct it was. I feel so foolish now!" She flashed her flirtatious smile at Stern as she feigned embarrassment at her blunder. "But I do remember the name the caller mentioned, sir. Do you happen to know which precinct is run by a Captain Falk?"

"Of course," Stern answered. "That's Sam Falk. He and I were classmates all the way back in high school. You know, he never could hit my curveball. That's the… umm…Nineteenth Precinct, Alice."

"Thank you, sir." Alice wrote the number 19 on her hand in red ink.

❖ ❖ ❖

As Captain Samuel Falk left the precinct for the evening, he had no idea that he was being watched from above. As he walked at a leisurely pace down the street upon which the stationhouse he commanded was located, he did not think to look up at the rooftops, for he had no cause for alarm or suspicion. Had he glanced skyward, he would have seen, silhouetted against the dimming dusk sky, a cloaked figure, clad all in black, slim and lithe and shapely, keeping pace with his homeward stroll by leaping from roof to roof along the avenue.

When Falk reached his house, his rooftop shadow paused as well, waiting for Falk to fish his keys from his pocket and unlock his door. As Falk went inside, the follower climbed down the building's wall and perched outside the window of the room in which a lamp had been lit. The eyes behind the red lace shroud peered through the window, watching as Falk poured himself a glass of brandy and sat down behind his desk and began going through the day's mail.

The window was slightly open due to the fairly warm weather, so the watcher outside the window soon became a listener as well when Falk's telephone began to ring. Falk took a sip of his drink and picked up the receiver.

"What?" the police captain barked rudely, unhappy at being bothered by the ringing telephone after just having arrived home for the night. "Oh…it's you again. What do you want, Jasper?"

Falk stopped talking, listened to the voice on the other end of the call. The figure outside the window waited, unable to hear what this "Jasper" was saying, for Falk to take his turn to speak again.

"I know you've been waiting a year, Jasper," said Samuel Falk. "I told you in the beginning, when you agreed to do the job, that it would take a while for me to get the money together. Look, you don't work cheap you know! I probably could have had that interfering whelp of a rookie taken out for a lot less than the five grand I owe you…but I couldn't trust anybody else. You've never botched a job, have you? What? What do you mean I could be the next job unless I pay up? Listen, you impudent fool! I'll have the entire force on your back if you don't hold your tongue! You'll have the money as soon as I have it!"

Falk slammed down the phone. He picked up his glass and downed the brandy in one gulp. He tossed most of the mail he had been sorting into the wastepaper basket beside the desk and stood up and left the room, angrily slamming the door shut as he walked out.

"Perfect timing," whispered the watcher as the one she watched went out of her sight.

The Red Veil reached into the partially open window. Her black-gloved hands pushed the window upward, increasing the size of the opening and she climbed inside the house. She looked around the small personal office of Captain Samuel Falk. The desk would be too vulnerable a place to hide any documents or other incriminating items. There had to be a hidden place, the Red Veil decided. She looked around, seeking anything suspicious or noteworthy. Her view, eyes gazing through the red-dyed gauzy material that covered her face, alighted on the wall. Yes, she decided, that one panel seems different, slightly lighter in color, off by just a fraction of shade. She walked over to the wall and tapped on the panel with the tip of a finger. Hollow!

The panel opened quite easily, not barred by any device, just well concealed in plain sight. Her hand reached into the small compartment and pulled forth a bundle of papers, tied together with twine. She sliced through the thin rope with one sharp talon, a claw constructed by the shearing of the badge of a fallen policeman, attached to the glove's finger in a moment of inspired morbidity. The twine snapped, cut easily by the razor on her hand. The papers fell loose and she rifled through them, tearing open envelopes and searching for anything of significance.

She read through a letter that had been stuck in the very middle of the pile. The name with which it was signed was a familiar one: Detective First Class Douglas Brown.

"Captain Falk, I accept your offer. It's quitting time then, I suppose. Don't worry about a thing. I won't say a word to anybody. As far as I'm concerned, I've never even heard your name. After all, you're not my precinct commander. I wash my hands of the case, completely. Just get those pension checks in the mail and I'll sit back and relax and forget the whole thing."

The Red Veil put the papers back into their nesting place and closed the panel in the wall. She walked out of the office room and into the hallway of Falk's home. The hall was dark and she could see no light ahead of her. She stopped and listened. The sound of running water met her ears.

She proceeded down the hallway until she saw a light on, the glow coming from under a door. She pressed her ear to the door. It was the sound of a shower, turned on, that she had heard.

Samuel Falk stood under the hot water, rinsing the soap from his body. The anger he had felt after the call from Jasper was beginning to subside as the shower washed away not only the soil on his body but the tension in his mind. He smiled to himself. So what if the hired killer was getting antsy about his payment? It didn't change the fact that they had gotten away with murder. Falk was smug, sure of himself, prideful.

He jumped as the sound of wood cracking roared over even the loudness of the water that rained down upon his shoulders in the shower. He tore open the shower curtain and found himself standing there, naked, dripping wet and vulnerable, face to face with a thing unlike any being he had ever seen before. He turned pale; he felt his heart begin to thump, louder and louder, harder and harder, inside his chest. It was a woman; a ghastly image of red and black and shadows that stood before him, long chestnut colored hair flowing out from behind a terrible red mask of gossamer webbing. Behind her, Falk could see the splintered remains of the bathroom door. How could a woman have broken the door like that, he wondered? Could any person as slim and small as that one, no matter how frightfully attired she was, have generated enough force to kick that door apart? What wrath had motivated such an action?

Falk backed up, his spine touching the wet shower wall. The nightmare woman took one step closer to him.

"Turn the water off!" she hissed in a voice that cut to the core of Falk's soul like a freshly honed scalpel.

He reached down and shut the shower off, pulling his wits together; reminding himself that he was a cop, and a tough old captain at that. "Who the hell are you? What kind of a getup is that? Are you insane waltzing in here like that?"

"You call me insane!" the Red Veil shrieked at Falk. "Perhaps I am. But a worse form of insanity is to prey upon the innocent and let evil deeds go unpunished. I see the need for justice on this night. In that sense, I am saner than you shall ever be."

"What do you want?" Falk roared.

The left hand of the Red Veil shot out from under her cloak. The speed was such that Samuel Falk did not even see the pistol or hear the shot ring out before he felt the terrible, shocking pain of the bullet ripping into his kneecap, smashing bone and letting loose blood that ran down his leg to mingle with the water that was still making its way down the drain. He fell to his uninjured knee and looked up at the shrouded face that mockingly stared down at him.

"What did Tommy Carter find out that made you hire a killer to murder him? You were up to something, weren't you, Falk? Corruption! What were you doing? Officer Carter stumbled onto you, didn't he? So you hired Jasper and you promised him money to kill Tommy and he lured Tommy to that apartment and shot him in cold blood! That's how it was, wasn't it, Falk? Wasn't it?"

"Yes!" Falk shouted back at the Red Veil, his rage and pain drowning out his fear. "That stupid kid couldn't take a hint. He would have blown his chances of ever moving up in the department, would have thrown away his career just to satisfy his childish sense of right and wrong. So what if I was taking a little on the side to see that some embezzlers and counterfeiters didn't get charges pressed against them? So what? But Carter overheard some stoolies talking about it and he started to snoop around and got a little too close. I had to take him out of the picture. I had no choice. Do you know what would have happened to me if they'd caught and convicted me? Do you know how many guys I put away before I made captain? Do you know what they'd do to me if I joined their cellblock? So the little rookie got shot! Big deal! He was just a little fish. I'm the big shark, you see? I'm still out here in the open seas!"

The Red Veil stared down at him, not speaking, not moving.

"What's it matter to you, anyway?" Falk said. It would be the last question he would ever ask.

The left hand put the gun back into the cloak. It reached up and lifted the veil from the face. A pair of bright blue eyes was revealed, containing a curious mixture of hatred and sorrow. The skin was like porcelain, the mouth twisted in a savage smile of bloodlust and grief. Falk was mesmerized by the unexpected beauty of the face that looked down at his pain-wracked body. He stared into those eyes and never knew the right hand had moved until he felt the talons cut into his throat and end his life.

❊ ❊ ❊

The man called Jasper sat on a barstool and stared at the day's paper. Two articles had caught his eye. He knew, though the writers of the pieces did not, he assumed, that the news in both was related. Captain Samuel Falk had been found brutally slain in his home, his throat slashed, his knee shattered by a shot. Also in the paper that day, a retired police detective, one Douglas Brown, had been committed to the city's primary mental hospital after breaking down and reporting being visited by a "terrible devil woman with a red face and black hide and claws as long as butcher knives." According to the paper, Brown had been under sedation after trying to throw himself off a rooftop so that "God could take me up to Heaven before that Bride of Satan drags me down to Hell."

Brown and Falk were connected. Of that, Jasper was sure. He was not a stupid man. After all, he'd killed at least a dozen men in his time, never been caught, and made a damn good living doing so. He credited himself as being a pretty smart fellow, clever enough to figure this situation out. Some crazy dame had dressed herself up in a creepy costume, visited Brown, found out about Falk, murdered him, and disappeared. Jasper figured it was a safe bet that whoever the dame was, she might come to see him next. He didn't want to take any chances; she might be a real psycho for all he knew.

He put down the paper, found a phone booth, popped some change in, and called for a few guys to watch his back for a few days. He knew enough people and was owed enough favors that it wasn't a hard task for him to round up some pretty decent hired muscle until things cooled down. He would wait in the bar, safety in numbers, among the crowd, until the boys showed up to escort him home. He felt inside his jacket for the comforting weight of his .45.

❊ ❊ ❊

The Syndicate had sent Milo, Cassius, and Bud. The three goons sat playing cards, smoking, and shooting the breeze while Jasper sat in the corner and thought. He had forbidden his three borrowed guards from drinking while on the job and that had caused them to be a bit grumpy, but they'd get over it when they received their tips, Jasper was certain. The three of them seemed to be enjoying the poker game and they were loud and jovial. Jasper was in the opposite mood; he didn't think his three companions understood the possible seriousness of the situation. He did. He was edgy, on the defensive, restless. He sat and listened to their thuggish banter and tried to think about the races, the last girl he'd spent the night with, the money he'd make on his next hit, or anything else, anything but what had happened to Captain Falk and that detective they'd locked up in the padded room. He knew he shouldn't have been so nervous. After all, who would even know where the little room they were hidden away in was located?

At just past midnight, a knock came on the door. Bud put down his cards and walked to the door, gun in hand. "Who's there?" he called out in his rough, backstreets voice.

The responding voice was drenched in honey, sweet, feminine, coy. "Are you the handsome fella who called for a little company tonight?"

Bud glanced back at his poker buddies. "I am now," he joked in their direction. His hand made contact with the doorknob.

Jasper was on his feet in an instant. "Bud, no! Don't open that..."

It was too late. The door swung open and the shot rang out. Bud's pistol dropped from his big hairy hand. The gun, unfired, hit the dirty, beer-stained carpet first, soon followed by the fresh carcass of Bud, a smoking hole ripped in his barrel-chest by the hot slug.

Milo and Cassius jumped up and stepped towards the door, then froze in their tracks, neither of them prepared for the vision of Hell-On-Two-Legs that greeted their stunned eyes. Milo raised his gun; Cassius lifted the steel pipe that he always kept close. Milo fired, but the Red Veil had executed a perfect stage fall, letting her body fall backwards and catching herself with her palms down as the bullet zinged over her head, harmlessly sailing through the open door and embedding itself in the wall across the corridor.

Before Milo could get another shot off, Cassius had charged ahead like a brazen bull, heading straight for the mystery woman who was now rising to her combat booted feet. She raised her cloak, tearing it loose from the fasteners that held it around her shoulders, throwing it over Cassius's head like a matador in action, blinding the big brute and slamming her hand, the clawed glove hand, into his ribs. The sound of those blades scraping bone made Jasper cringe from across the room. Cassius fell.

Milo fired again. The bullet came closer this time, ripping through the blackened lace of the wedding gown that had become the Red Veil's guise. It missed the tender flesh, though she could feel the heat of the projectile as it singed her shoulder. A second round left her pistol and ended the career, and the life, of the hired gun called Milo.

Jasper stood alone in the corner. He stared intensely at the veiled figure that advanced in his direction. Then he glanced away and realized that he had left his jacket, still containing his gun, hung over the back of the chair that sat, waiting and taunting him, ten feet away. He watched the Red Veil aim at his chest, but she hesitated. She tossed her gun onto the floor and raised her now empty hand to her face, tearing off the crimson shroud that covered her countenance. The blue eyes flashed in Jasper's direction. The ruby lips smiled sweetly but dangerously.

"Hello, Jasper. My name is Alice, and I'm going to kill you."

Jasper's hand dropped to his side as he bent his knee to bring his ankle up to meet his hand. In a blur of skill, practiced a thousand times in preparation for such a

The door swung open and the shot rang out.

moment of desperation, he produced a long dagger from its concealment in his pants leg. He let out a battle cry of pompous ferocity and charged at Alice, dagger flashing wildly from side to side, intent on gutting her where she stood.

Jasper advanced, Alice dodged. She tried to spin around and catch him with her clawed glove, but he was too fast, too experienced a fighter, too skilled a killer. She missed. She felt a sudden pain in her forearm as Jasper drew first blood. She glanced down. Red ran from out of her sleeve and dripped onto the floor, but it was just a trickle, only a surface wound, no need to panic. She backed up, Jasper coming at her again. He slashed at her, she dodged this time. She swung the taloned hand back to try to generate speed and force for a killing strike, but she misjudged the room she had to maneuver in; the glove struck the wall, the improvised attachments broke loose, and the five claws made from the remnants of the shorn badge fell away; she was disarmed.

Jasper struck again, narrowly missing Alice's jugular. Careful, Alice, careful, she warned herself. She ducked as the dagger flashed over her head. The advantage, she realized fearfully, belonged to Jasper now. It was only her agility that had kept the last two moves from cutting her to the bone.

Alice's mind flashed back, as it had so often since she had begun to engage in her strangely costumed nocturnal escapades, to the rough years she had spent on the East End, watching the street brawlers and avoiding both the rape gangs and the authorities. Go low, her instincts told her. She kicked her feet out in front of her body, letting gravity take hold of her and fell into a seated position on the floor, a jarring impact but a well executed move. She placed her hands on the floor at her sides and spun around, legs sweeping out and kicking the balance out from underneath Jasper. He began to fall, his face coming down and plummeting toward Alice's. She could see his eyes, red with rage and bloodlust. She rolled clear of his falling body. He landed flat on his stomach, the dagger still in his outstretched hand.

Alice stood, springing to her feet like a cat. She brought her heavy, thick-soled boot down on Jasper's hand, breaking his fingers and his grip on the knife. The hired killer cried out in agony.

Alice stood there and looked down at the pathetic creature on the floor. There he was: Tommy's killer, at her mercy. She thought of the ways in which she could end Jasper's life. Which would satisfy her lust for revenge the best? Rage and hate for that man flashed in her eyes until, suddenly, something stopped that train of thought. In her memory's eye she could see Tommy, tall and handsome and alive. She could see him polishing his badge and cleaning his gun and heading off to walk his beat and protect the innocent and see that justice was done and always do the right thing. What would he have done had he been hunting for her murderer?

"I should cut you to pieces where you lay," Alice hissed at Jasper. "I should slice you once for every person you've killed and then start over at one and do it all over again. But I'm not going to do that. I'm not even going to kill you quickly. You won't die tonight. They'll come and take you and lock you up for a long time. Maybe you'll sit in the electric chair, but that's not up to me. But remember this, Jasper. You may know who I am…but you also know what I'm capable of. You won't tell anyone who

I am, no matter what kind of deal they offer you, no matter how much you think that information might save your life. If you do, I'll find a way to get to you no matter how deep down in the solitary cells they hide you, and when I get there I will make you wish you'd never killed a single human being, wish you'd never taken a job for Samuel Falk, wish you'd never even been born. Understand that, Jasper. You won't tell anyone who I am. And remember this too: I'm letting you live because Tommy would have let you live. Think about that. The man you killed just saved your life. Just think about that."

Jasper heard no more, for a kick to the side of his head sent him on a long trip into unconsciousness. He would wake up days later, locked up, where he would spend the remainder of his wasted life.

Alice picked up her crimson veil from the floor. She put it back over her face, for she knew that her voice sounded different when filtered through that lace mask. She picked up the room's telephone.

"Hello," said Edward Stern. His voice was half asleep to match the rest of him. As a lifelong police officer, he was used to getting calls in the middle of the night, but that never made it easier to have a good sleep abruptly halted. "Who's there?"

Much to Stern's surprise, it was a woman's voice that he heard. It had a strange timbre, an oddness that made him uneasy, but he listened with interest to what that voice had to tell him.

"Captain Stern. I have a gift for you at 2727 East Fiftieth Street, Apartment Five-Fifteen. It should clear up a handful of old cases that are still open…and might even make you reopen some that were prematurely closed."

"Thank you…Miss…" Stern paused. "I didn't get your name. Will you tell me your name?"

The voice on the line laughed. Stern couldn't tell if the laughter was sweet and girlish or crazed and wicked. Perhaps he heard a little bit of both qualities in that strange laughter. The voice spoke once more before Stern heard the click of the call's termination.

"If I must have a name…The Red Veil will suffice."

The End

A CREATURE OF LIGHT AND DARKNESS
An Essay by Aaron Smith

Yes, the title of this essay is indeed a reference to Roger Zelazny's novel, Creatures of Light and Darkness, which I just discovered is finally back in print after a long, long time. It's a great novel, unlike anything else I've ever read and I'd recommend it to anyone who likes good science-fantasy with mythological symbolism. I just happened to be thinking of it when I sat down to write this essay and realized that the character I've just finished writing about, the Red Veil, is indeed a creature of light and darkness, a character with two distinct looks, different as night and day, different as love and hate, a being of two opposing personalities and two very different demeanors.

Ron Fortier, the editor of Airship 27's line of pulp anthologies had put out the call for someone to create what he called a "mystery woman," the female equivalent of those cloaked and mysterious and ruthless and dangerous pulp heroes like the Shadow and the Spider. At the time, I had just begun work on a new novel which has not yet been completed, or even progressed very far, as I write this. The novel, a horror story, was going to be the first time I'd written anything with a female lead character. I was certain that that would be a bit different than writing about a male lead. So, I took the challenge of coming up with this "female Shadow" to sharpen my pen a little before I even introduced my female protagonist in the other project.

Now, I had to bear in mind that the pulp story Ron needed, like most of Airship 27's output, would have to be set in the 1930s. It's a little different writing a female character in that era than it is in a modern setting. In today's society, in the world of 2010, a woman is, for the most part; free to engage in almost any profession that a man can. In a modern setting, no one would doubt the authenticity of having a female police officer or military officer or private investigator or any other role that would have, in the Thirties, been considered a man's job. The same holds true for pulp heroes. Sure, there were female pulp heroines like the Domino Lady for example, but as far as I know (not that my knowledge of pulps is as extensive as some of my Airship colleagues) there had not been one as ruthless or frightening to criminals or outright violent and deadly as the Spider or the Black Bat.

So who, I began to wonder, would this woman be? What would be her motivation? Why would she don a disguise and go off into the shadows of the city and mercilessly hunt down those who did evil? I thought of the last story I had had released by

Airship 27. It was a western featuring Wild Bill Hickok and the primary theme of the story was revenge. Revenge always works.

I also thought of World War II and how, with so many young men off fighting and dying in Europe and the Pacific, it often fell to the women left behind to fill the factory jobs and other jobs that had been the domain of men before the war took them away.

So, I decided, our mystery woman would have to step into a role vacated by a man, with revenge or, to phrase it more positively, justice as her guiding motivation. I came up with poor young Alice Carter, widow of a slain young policeman; finding herself suddenly alone and, to make matters worse, without any closure, any understanding of what forces had led to her husband being taken away from her.

Love is taken away from Alice, and then the authorities, those who people THINK they can count on to help them in times of need, turn their backs on Alice and her need to find answers. That would send anyone into a spiraling descent into grief and anger and borderline insanity. At that point, I suspect, one might very well end up in a permanent state of depression, rage, and mental imbalance. The trick is to know when to stop the downward slide and turn that angry energy into something useful and even constructive. Alice Carter does that…and the Red Veil is born.

A broken heart, an unavenged murder, unanswered questions, a police badge cut to shreds by a bereaved widow, a wedding dress dyed crimson and black, a childhood that taught a young girl to fend for herself when need be, a corruption within the police department, a dual personality, and an image designed to scare the pants off any criminal who crosses Alice's path! I threw all these ingredients into the cauldron and the Red Veil was born!

I had an absolute blast writing this one. There's a wonderful beauty in this woman scorned and I don't think she's done confronting evil yet. I hope you enjoy this first tale of the Red Veil and I hope you'll come back for more when I write another one. If I have my way, the Red Veil will be haunting the waking dreams of New York's underworld for a long time to come.

As I look back at the writing of "Hell Hath No Fury…" I can see some of the creators that went before me who have influenced me in this project. There's a little of the Universal Horror movies in there; maybe that's where the image of the costume that I had in my head came from. I am also, of course, indebted to those who created the Shadow and the Spider and the Black Bat and even Batman for creating the template upon which the Red Veil is, to some extent, modeled. And I should also mention the great HBO television series Rome. In an episode of the show's first season, the character of Servilia, normally a composed, serene woman of high social standing, becomes so enraged by certain injustices done to her that she kneels before an altar, enacts a rite of vengeance form the Roman civilization's religion, and sits there, in a voice so full of anger and hate and power as to render its sound almost otherworldly, she proceeds to lay a curse upon those who have wronged her, imploring various gods of the inferno to exact revenge upon them. That chilling performance by actress Lindsay Duncan was certainly in the back of my mind when I wrote the scenes where Alice speaks not with her usual voice, but as the Red Veil.

So my story set in the 1930s was partially influenced by a TV show from the 2000's that was set two thousand years in the past. It's strange how those things work out.

❖ ❖ ❖

AARON SMITH - has had stories published in numerous books from Airship 27 Productions. His work has appeared in *Sherlock Holmes Consulting Detective Volume 1, Dan Fowler G-Man Volume 1, Lance Star Sky Ranger Volume 2, The Masked Rider Volume 1,* and the novel *Season of Madness.*

He is the creator of The Red Veil and Hound Dog Harker. He has also written a science fiction novel, *Gods and Galaxies.*

Gridiron
"First Down"
By David Boop

Gridiron /grid,ī(ə)rn/ (n) - *a hunk of metal used to heat things up.*

Now

He awoke to pain. He was the pain and the pain was him. He'd known physical pain, had caused it, but not like this. This he couldn't control, as he'd done so many times in the past. There was no drug, no workout, no therapy for the pain. He could, however, give the pain a voice and so he raged until the pain went away and the rage was all that was left.

❈ ❈ ❈

Sharky wasn't a clever nickname by any stretch of the imagination. A loan shark by trade, he felt coming up with a cleverer nickname was a waste of time better spent on separating rubes from their money. When someone came to Sharky for a loan, they knew exactly what they were getting into, so he never listened to the whiners and complainers.

"I'm a shark," he'd say when a client would beg for mercy, "I've got to eat."

As he closed up his deli on Third, he considered giving the front up once again, as it took time away from the real moola. The local mob was taking a bigger and bigger cut of his action and the store itself wasn't doing all that great. He had inventories to keep up and, as it was, he kept some of his stock in the case longer than recommended. That'd be all he'd need; someone to get sick or die; then all that rainy day money he'd squirreled away would be gone.

After the door was locked and the sign turned off, Sharky took the cash drawer to the back. He opened the safe, stuck the whole tray in, and looked at the piles of Franklins above it. He wished for a moment he could just take a stack and run, but he knew there was no place in the world he could hide from The Giordanos. He was better off just trying to reduce his losses and plan for an early retirement.

The back door shattered in a million pieces as something came through it. Sharky ducked as shards of wood rained over him. He reached for the gun he had hidden in the safe for just such emergencies. He had the gun out, and reflex taking over, fired without even thinking. Six bullets unloaded into a hulking shape standing just on his side of the doorway, yet the thing still stood there. He dropped the piece and slid a holdout from inside his boot. He fired again, but the bullet just bounced off and shattered a nearby lamp.

The room went dark, save for the light from the alleyway, casting the man-mountain in an eerie glow; its massive form a terrible visage of ruthlessness. Sharky cowered into a corner of the room as it advanced.

"What do you want?" Sharky croaked, "Take the money, it's not mine."

"I know."

The voice carried with it the misery of a life gone wrong. It was empty of joy and concern.

"Then you know what'll happen, right? You won't get away with taking the mob's money. The Giordanos; they'll come for you!"

"I hope so."

The man-shaped being pulled out a can of lighter fluid from under his massive midnight cloak. He sprayed the contents into the safe, making sure he coated all the dough inside. With his sizeable hand, he reached over and lifted Sharky off the floor. With the other, he struck a match against Sharky's desk. The loan man screamed and tried to free himself, but the monster's gauntlet was too strong.

"Tell your masters about this. Tell them their love of money will be their downfall."

The giant tossed Sharky through the smashed door after dropping the match by the safe. The inferno was a fury of flames, hungrily devouring the money and engulfing the room in moments. In a pile of alley trash, Sharky watched as his life burned. The creature stepped back into the alley and Sharky could see exposed skin absorbing light like an iron pot over a campfire. Cold metal reflected a steamy rage. In place of a mouth was a half-mask sporting Satan's smile. Words like curses came from under it.

"Tell them," the thing that was once a man said, "That Gridiron is coming."

Six months ago

Gordon "Gory" Burrell struck a match on the side of his locker. He had about thirty seconds to inhale the smoke from his cancer stick before he'd have to stub it out and get on the field. He let the smoke fill his lungs until his head swam, then crushed the cigarette on the floor. Gory grabbed his old familiar helmet, the leather worn from sweat and abuse so that it fit his head just right. They offered him new ones, but why when his head was harder than any skull since the cavemen. He'd go without it all together, if the refs would let him.

He walked down the long hallway towards the field, always the last one out. Of all his teammates, Gory was the only one dedicated to full-time professional football and liked a few moments of contemplation before the game started.

Two men in suits waited for him about halfway down.

"Hey, Gory. You've got quite a record out there."

Fans. Nice. "Thanks. Gotta go play ball. If you'd like, I can sign something for you after the game."

The one who spoke laughed. It was sinister, like a hyena in the jungle. A toothpick hung loosely on his lips, but didn't drop even during his outburst. "Listen to him, would ya, Axe? 'Sign something,' he says!"

The other man nodded and said, "Sure, Pick. He said that." Man of few words, he was about as big as Gory out of uniform. He just stared the linebacker down from under his fedora. Gory got the idea who these guys were.

"Okay, Mack," explained the talkative one, "This is how it's going to go down. You're going to have an off day. You're going to let them rushers get through enough that the score is going to favor the other team. Nothing too obvious. For your troubles, you'll get a nice little present off-season. Keep it up and we'll see you never have to take a hit in the head again."

Gory didn't have time for this. "Not interested."

He tried to continue on his way, but the big guy impeded his path.

"'Not interested,' he says," repeated the skinny one, "Listen, buddy. You get paid peanuts as it is, and we know you've got a dame you're hot under the collar to marry. Don't you want to do that in style?"

Just the thought of them using June as leverage brought to all the thunder Gory took to the field to bear. He punched Pick, sending him sprawling against the tunnel wall. He slumped down the stone, toothpick never leaving his mouth. Before Axe could react, Gory had grabbed him between the legs, twisting the man's heritage and bringing him to his knees. To finish him off, he slammed both hands against the sides of his neck, making sure the muscle man wouldn't be getting up soon. He raised Pick up off the ground so he was staring the mob's mouthpiece directly eye to eye.

"Don't ever come around here again, and if you come anywhere near my family, what he got will seem merciful."

Dropping him to the ground, Gory went to the gridiron, ready to vent on an unsuspecting opponent.

Now

June White saw the flashing light before she heard the buzz. It was her goal to get calls connected before the alarm sounded. Her reflexes were getting so good, that barely a buzz— went off before she answered, "Everett Herald, where the good people of Everett get their news first. How may I connect your call?"

She never sounded bored. "Each time is like the first time you've spoken it," complimented her supervisor. June liked her job, not just because it helped her take care of her daughter, April, but because she liked to be in the know. Everything that happened in the sprawling metropolis of Everett, California came through the grapevine here. Plus, the daily grind kept her mind off the ache in her heart. It'd been months since Gordon's disappearance.

Terry Johnston slid up beside her desk, smiling that puppy-dog smile he thought

"Okay, Mack. This is how it's going to go down. You're going to have an off day."

was irresistible. Maybe to others, but June was not falling for it.

When she caught a break between calls, she addressed him, "Hello Terrance."

He sighed. "Come on, June. Why can't you call me 'Pointer' like everyone else does."

She raised an eyebrow. "That's because no one else calls you that. Just you."

He leaned across her desk and his blue eyes flashed with ambition. "That's only because I haven't cracked a big story yet. You just watch! I'll get the scoop and they'll all say, 'Hey! That Pointer, he sure knows where the action is.' Then I'll get off the sports beat and onto the crime beat."

June transferred a call before turning back to him, "It's nice to have a goal, Terrance, but you're a good sports reporter. I don't see why you're not happy with that?"

He slumped a little, "Well, I can't rightly ask you to marry me on a sports reporter's salary, can I? When I'm making the big bucks, then you'll see that I'm an upstanding sort of Joe who'll take care of his dame."

She was flattered, as she always was by his awkward come-ons, but she wasn't ready to move forward. "I'm sorry, but I've already lost two men in my life. I'm not ready to start down the road with another. Certainly not until I hear why Gordon left so suddenly."

He snapped his fingers, "That's right! I heard something about your wayward fiancé."

She nearly jumped over the desk, her chair careening back. "What? What have you heard? Is he alive?"

Pointer waved her down, trying to calm her. "Nothing like that, sugar. It's just that this bookie I know, one tied with you-know-who?" He winked. June understood. The Giordanos had grown stronger in the recent years, monopolizing Everett's underworld and getting their dirty fingers even into some of the higher offices of city hall... if rumors were to be believed. "Someone did a number on him and now he's in General taking his breakfast through a tube."

"Poor man, but how does that tie into Gordon?"

"Well, this bookie was the one that had carried the mob's bet on that game that Gory—" he corrected himself, "Sorry, Gordon wouldn't throw."

That game. Everything in her life changed because of that game. She lay awake at night, debating whether Gordon should have just thrown it. He was a good man, better than she'd ever met, and she loved that he took a stand against the mob, but if he had just taken the dive, he'd not have left town; a shattered remnant of the man he once was.

"So do you think this was some sort of payback from his bosses?"

Pointer shook his head, "Nah, that's the crazy thing. He said he was beat up by a monster. The police thought he said 'mobster' and got all excited, thinking they finally had a stoolie, but he kept shaking his head and finally wrote it down. The description was to-the-moon insane. The coppers think he's got some sort of brain damage, but there's more."

June was torn between the tale Terrance spun and her duties. Something felt tight, in the pit of her stomach. She didn't know what, something other than the connection to Gordon. She looked at the clock. She had a break coming up and told Terrance to meet her at the coffee shop across the street. That way she'd be able to focus without all the hullabaloo of the phones.

"It's not a date," she had to clarify once she saw his beaming smile, "Just a talk about your information."

"See, this isn't the first Family connected guy to end up in a full body cast. There was Sharky the loan shark, about three weeks ago, too."

"Original name," quipped June.

"Yeah, there's a story there, but another time. It's connected to the bookie like this; Sharky's front, a deli, gets torched and, of course, everyone thought he'd crossed the mob somehow, but scuttlebutt says the mob's money was in it when it went up. And this jockey I know says Sharky was at the track, drinking like fish in the desert, face bandaged, arm in a sling, and ramblin' about some behemoth that did the deed."

June could see where he was going now. "So, you think the two incidents are connected? Did either guy give a description?"

"That's why the cops won't take the bookie serious, and Sharky's on the outs with the mob. Their description of the thing is straight out of the funny papers."

She leaned in conspiratorially, "And?"

Terry had her hooked and was deciding whether to reel her in. He leaned back, arm slung over the back of the booth in a smooth savoir-faire way. "I don't know, Doll Face. Maybe this info shouldn't be shared. It could mean my big break, and I really shouldn't spill it to anyone I'm not intimately associated with."

June was faster than he could have imagined. Her hand shot out and grabbed his necktie. She pulled him over the table and got in his face. "I'm not your doll, and I'll never be your doll if you keep making 'jokes' like that. Okay, Mister Johnson?"

He gasped for breath as his necktie became a garrote. Terry nodded his head and June let go. She sat back smiling knowing Terry would be mighty careful in the future or lose her trust altogether. He loosened his tie and cleared his throat. He squeaked on the first couple of words, but regained his voice.

"They said, er, they said the thing was shaped like a man, a large man, but had skin like metal; iron to be specific. It was dressed in a massive trench coat the color of evil itself. It wore a weird mask over the lower part of its face, shaped like a menacing grin. Its eyes were cold and held no emotion except anger. And when it talked, it talked like a voice from the grave."

Later that night, after putting April to bed, June shivered in her kitchen, despite it being summer and still 85 degrees out. The description Terrance gave made her scared all over again. If such a thing was out there, it wasn't natural. But then, the thought of it attacking only mob guys gave her pause. Maybe it had its reasons. And anything, June realized with morbid fascination, that hurt The Giordanos made her happy.

Could this thing be all that bad?

Five months ago

Gory finished putting the dishes in the sink and stated running water. June admonished him.

"Gordon, you don't need to do that. You just finished the season yesterday. You've got to be tired. I'll do them."

He blocked her from reaching the sink. She tried to dart left, then right, but despite his massive bulk, he was too quick for her. "You did all the work cooking and serving, Doll Face. This one's on me. You go relax in the other room with April."

She faked him one last time, but only to get in close for a hug. He wrapped her in his tree trunk limbs and carefully hugged back.

"How'd I get so lucky?" they both said in unison, then laughed. April peeked into the kitchen and giggled at the sight. Her mom turned just in time to see her Shirley Temple curls dart back out of sight.

"Okay, Mister. You win this time, but don't make a habit of it. I like to spoil you. You get too many people who want to break you on the field. I just want to pamper you when you come over."

Gory started his task, speaking over his shoulder, "Oh, you've broken me, alright. I'm like a wild mustang who's now more comfortable in the stable."

June liked that, thinking he was more comfortable here. Once he got his end-of-season pay, they'd run off to the courthouse and get married. She'd had the big wedding once and he didn't seem to mind. April loved him, and he her, so the sooner they got hitched, the better impression it'd make on her, give her a daddy again. She barely remembered her real daddy now, only seeing him in dreams occasionally. Since Gordon had entered their lives, the ten year old was more alive than June could ever remember.

After listening to Burns and Allen, Gory gave his sweetness a short but promising kiss goodnight. April safely tucked in bed, June watched from the window as her future husband hailed a taxi. As it pulled away, she thought she caught movement in the back seat, but it was out of sight too quickly.

She figured she'd just ask him about it tomorrow.

Now

Antonio "Big Papa" Giordano couldn't believe his own ears.

"Charlie! Come here! Please tell me there's some clam sauce or something stuck in my ears because I could not have heard this dead man clearly."

Charlie, Big Papa's nephew approached the patriarch and carefully looked in the old man's right ear. "Nothing there, Big Papa."

Big Papa turned from his seat at the head of the enormous table he sat at and cuffed Charlie upside the head. "Doofus! That was one of those rhetorical questions. Can't you tell the difference? Geez, Louise. A million schmoes out of work and I get this one." Charlie slinked back to his corner just off center from his boss.

Pick gave his hyena-like chortle, while his partner Axe stood stone-faced as always. The man in front of Big Papa tried to smile, however it came out more as a grimace having locked onto the "dead man" comment. The mob boss's two enforcers kept him on his knees.

Big Papa readdressed the penitent man, "So, you really want me to believe, once again, that some sort of monster is trying to single-handedly destroy my empire? Choose your next words carefully, as they will make the difference to your future within this organization."

The man, a low level pimp in The Giordanos's hierarchy, swallowed hard and told his story once again. "I swear to you on my life, Big Papa, a guy as big as a mountain busted through the doors on my hotel. He smashed my counter like it was Lincoln Logs. I grabbed my shotgun and I unloaded a round right square in the chest. I swear on my mother's grave," the man crossed himself, "the guy didn't even flinch. His jacket and shirt were blown away and I could see his skin. It was metal."

"You mean he had some sort of steel shirt underneath his clothes?"

The pimp shook his head, "No, Big Papa. His skin, it was metal. It moved and flexed as he did. I've never seen nothing like it."

"Tell him what you told me," Pick said, a mad glee in his eyes.

"He said he had a message for you, Big Papa."

Big Papa leaned forward expectantly, "And that message?"

Again, the man swallowed. He looked at Pick, looked at Axe, hoping to see some sort of reprieve in their expressions. No help coming, the man gave up the ghost.

"He said to tell you he was getting closer. Gridiron was getting closer to you."

The Patriarch sat back in his oversized chair, fingers laced across his massive gut. He closed his eyelids, but the eyes beneath moved rapidly, as if he was experiencing a nightmare. Without opening them, he lurched forward and, with a massive meat-hook, slammed all the plates filled with pasta to the floor with a thunderous crash. Charlie and the pimp both reeled back in surprise, but the Enforcers were stoic in their places.

"Get this peon out of here!"

Axe, so named as he was the man Big Papa called on when he had an axe to grind, grabbed the purveyor of flesh by the collar and dragged him from the room. Big Papa steamed, his breath escaping from the snarl on his face. "That's three, Pick. Three! Somebody's got a death wish if he thinks he can mess with The Giordanos and get away with it. I want this thing, this Gridiron. I want it dead. And not just dead, Pick. I want it chopped to pieces if you have to take a blowtorch to him. I want to know who its people are. Cut them into little pieces, too."

Pick loved this type of assignment because he got to be creative. "Whatever you say, Big Papa. This will be fun."

The mobster calmed down, knowing his enforcers would take care of this menace. "Nobody messes with my family... Nobody!"

Four months ago

June sat at Gordon's bedside and looked at her fiancé for the umpteenth time, hoping to see movement. And for the umpteenth time, there was only the rise and fall of his chest. The continued noise of his labored breath through the oxygen mask was the only comfort she drew from the situation. As long as he breathed, there was hope he'd wake. It'd been a month since the mob took Gordon right from her doorstep. Maybe if she'd acted faster, the police would have rescued him before they did their devil's work. She'd live with that guilt forever and only hoped she could make it up to him when he came out of his coma.

She could hear the police officer guard snoring in the hallway. Some help he'd be if Big Papa sent any of his enforcers to finish the job they started. He was really just there to report when Gordon awoke more than for any serious protection. Federal agents had already questioned her. Now they wanted to grill Gordon as soon as he woke up. They would give him no time to grieve, no time to think. They wanted his raw reaction when he woke and saw what shape the mob had left him in. June was sure they thought he'd immediately tell them everything and they could bring down Big Papa once and for all.

But June had learned a lot at the paper; most of it from Mr. Johnson, Terrance, the sports reporter and a friend of Gordon's.

"They let him live for a reason," Terry had sagely spoke while they both sat vigil, "They want him as an example to other athletes that when Big Papa says 'dive,' you dive!"

"But what if he wakes up and remembers who did this to him, Terry? Won't he go to the police?" An increasing tremble in June's voice came with each question, "What if they kill him before he can go to trial?"

Terry had put his hand on her shoulder, "I doubt he'll talk to the police or the Feds. The other reason they let him live is they're sure he won't squeal."

June looked confused, and Terry's face pained as he told her what he suspected. "Gordon has a blind spot, hon'. They beat that weakness into him, made sure that if he woke he'd remember it. Gordon knows that if the mob can get to him, they can get to... you."

Terry was right, and June felt even guiltier that she might be a weight around this good man's neck. She might be the one that brought the mighty warrior down, like some Greek tragedy. June accepted the fact that they would be cowards. They'd run away together, all three of them, and start over someplace. Gordon would find a different line of work, as would she. They'd focus on love and put all this mob stuff behind them.

A groan slipped quietly from Gordon's lips, nearly unheard beneath the oxygen mask. June listened closely to make sure she hadn't misheard. A second louder noise, this one with feeling, followed the first.

"Gordon? Gordon? Can you hear me?"

There was nothing to substantiate the noise, at first, but then came an almost imperceptible twitch of his hand. Little movements followed; his eyelids, fingers, shoulders. It was like a house warming up floor by floor, room by room. Gordon's eyes opened a crack then shut again, pinched against the pain of light. June closed the blinds so only a fraction of daylight leaked in.

She tried again, "Gordon? It's me, darling. It's June. I'm here"

June debated getting a nurse. She knew as soon as she did, the circus would start. She wanted to be alone with him for a few moments first.

"If you can hear me, squeeze my hand."

With very little strength in his mitts, Gory gave her a squeeze.

"Good. Now, don't try to talk yet. You've been asleep for a long time and your voice will be hoarse. Just listen. Before I get the doctors, I want you to know something."

He squeezed her hand again. This was the moment. She steeled herself and leaned in close.

"I know what they did to you, my love, and it doesn't matter. I love you just the same. You're alive and back with me. We'll find a way to adjust. Just know, I will be with you, forever."

A tear dripped from Gordon's still clenched eyelids. The pain of his injuries, the pain of remembering, it must be tearing him up inside.

"And I know what they must have told you. Big Papa probably threatened me or maybe even said he'd hurt April, right? But we'd be okay if you didn't testify."

Gordon didn't say anything, but his breathing increased.

"Well, I've time to think about it, and I want you to know how I feel."

She leaned in even closer to his ear, so that her lips touched them, and whispered, "Make them pay, Gory. Make those bastards pay."

When she leaned back, Gordon "Gory" Burrell's eyes were wide open. June smiled down at him with trust and affection. His eyes softened and relaxed. Then, he too, gave a knowing smile back.

Now

The Everett Herald bullpen meeting was never what anyone viewing would call orderly. The Chief yelled out to reporters telling them where they were going and which shutterbug to take with them.

"Clausen? You're down to the Mayor's office regarding the new water treatment plant. Don't leave until you get a yes or no from him. I don't want him sitting on this until after the election. Take Elmer with you. See if he can find some polluted water to snap."

With a quick, "Got it, Chief," Clausen was out the door.

This continued down the list and Pointer was getting restless. It was one thing to not give him the assignment despite all the reports he'd brought the Chief, but to just not cover it, well, that was un-American. He couldn't take it anymore.

"Chief?" Pointer shouted, "What about the Gridiron reports? Who ya going to assign to it?"

All turned to their boss, whose eyes burned with a fire of embarrassment and rage. Not wanting to make a scene, he brought his temper down and addressed the sports writer.

"Oh, we're calling it 'Gridiron' now, are we? Why not Bigfoot? Or the Martian Man?"

This brought a chuckle from his staff, which helped with the Chief's attitude. Pointer was not to be dissuaded.

"I got it from a tip from a guy who knows another guy who's sister to the bookie that got squashed. It was the only word the police got out of the guy before he went back unconscious. So, that's on the official police report."

"Okay, Johnson. Let me get this straight. We're dealing with the worse collapse of industry since the country started, mob violence running wild, and people whispering war in Europe and you want the paper to spend what little money we have on chasing the boogie man?"

The Chief was hoping to belittle the reporter into slinking away, but Pointer was ready for it. "But that's just the thing, Chief. It is bad out there. And the government, and the cops, they can't or aren't doing enough to make it better. Then, out of the darkness comes this thing out of someone's nightmare."

Pointer looked around and saw that he had everyone's attention. He had his moment and it was now or never. He pulled out a chair and stepped onto it.

"But it's not out of some kid's nightmare, no! It's out of Big Papa's!"

"I heard," shouted one editor, "That he's ten feet tall!"

Another chimed in, "I heard he can fly!"

"This girl I know saw him," added a secretary, "and she said he wasn't even human! That he walked like a man, but his face was like Frankenstein's!"

"This thing," cut in Pointer, wanting to get the focus back on himself, "man, beast, whatever, is single-handedly dismantling The Giordanos. He's shut down half a dozen mob fronts, put two dozen criminals in the hospital or behind bars. Big Papa keeps offering bigger and bigger bounties on his head, but no one's even come close to hurting him."

The reporter crouched down on his haunches, "People are talking about him, that he is some sort of demon, but I say, no. He is not a demon. He is a vengeful angel. That's why bullets bounce off of him. He is exactly what the people need; an unstoppable force."

Standing up again, Terry "Pointer" Johnson pointed his finger towards the grand city out the window and with conviction said, "They need a hero! Let's give them one!"

The assembly broke out in applause and whistles of support. Even the Chief had to laugh. "Okay, 'Pointer,' you've made your point. You can have the Gridiron story."

"Yes!"

"BUT," continued the Chief, "you still have to cover sports and you're not getting a cent more per word." Under his breath, he said, "Not unless it sells papers."

Pointer jumped down from his chair and shook the Chief's hand, "Yessir, you won't regret it, sir!"

He spun around and spotted Massey, their newest and least experienced photographer. "Massey, you're with me. We're going to go catch us a gargoyle."

Three Months ago

"**M**r. Burrell, can you again recount the events of the night in question?"

The D.A. cast a quick glance over to the jury, several of which he was sure Big Papa had already gotten to. They appeared nervous and sweaty. Almost all looked like they'd rather be somewhere else. Doing your civic duty might get you lunch for a week, but it wouldn't put food on the table. The attorney was sure Big Papa offered them more than that. His only hope would be that the severity of the crime might stir something in these twelve people to convict Big Papa's enforcers and maybe then the feds could get them to turn state's evidence on the patriarch himself with racketeering charges.

All the prep work; from convincing the police to arrest Pick and Axe, to working with the FBI, to convincing a judge to give them a speedy trial before too much got in the papers and Big Papa could reach all the jurors, meant nothing. Everything hinged on Gory's testimony.

Gory cleared his throat, took a drink of water, and from the stand told the story he'd told a dozen people since he began his crusade.

"I'd just left my fiancé's apartment and hailed a cab. When I got in, I didn't notice, at first, that there were two other men in the car."

"Are those two men in the courtroom today, sir?"

"Yes."

"And can you point them out to the jury?"

Gordon pointed to where Pick and Axe sat in their defendant's seats.

"Please make a note in the records that Mr. Burrell pointed to Patrick 'The Pick' Ziegler and Axel 'The Axe' Acciaroli."

The court reporter made the note, looking as nervous as the jury did. This is the closest the City had ever gotten to Big Papa and whether directly or indirectly, he'd made it known that if his enforcers went down, there would be payback.

"What happened in the taxi?"

"The skinny one..."

"Patrick?"

"Yeah, weasel face."

This got a chuckle from a couple people, who then looked shameful afterwards.

"He draws a gun from the front seat. His troll partner..."

"Axel?"

"The troll covers my mouth with a towel soaked in some smelly fluid."

"Chloroform?"

The defense lawyer stood up, "Objection! Leading the witness!"

Gory ignored him and rapidly got his thought out, "Whatever. I'm trying to push him off me, but next thing I know, I'm getting sleepy." The judge reprimanded Gory and the prosecutor, who said they'd do better. "I wake up sometime later, tied to a board."

"Did you know where you were?"

"No idea. Some warehouse. There was nothing to identify it on the ceiling."

"And you couldn't move around?"

"Nah, they had every part of me strapped down. I was tied up worse than a bank loan."

There were scattered chuckles again. The D.A. liked that. If they liked Gory better than they feared Big Papa, they all stood a chance.

"Could you see anyone?"

"Yeah, that mug with his magic toothpick."

"Patrick?"

"Yes."

"Did Patrick talk to you?"

"Yeah, but he didn't say much. Just one thing, really."

The attorney raised his voice just a few octaves to make sure the jury knew that this was important, "And what did he say, Mr. Burrell?"

"Weasel-boy said, with that little hyena-like laugh of his, 'You should have no trouble taking a dive after this.'"

"Referring to the request he made of you in the tunnel before the football game, as you testified earlier?"

"Yes."

"And that's when you saw Axel?"

"Objection!" shouted the defense attorney, and whined about a leash.

"Sustained," agreed the judge.

"What happened next, Mr. Burrell?"

"The big ape came into view."

"Axel?"

"Yes, Axel."

"Did you notice anything odd about him?"

"Yes."

"And what was that, Mr. Burrell?"

"The sledgehammer he was holding."

There was a collective gasp. After Gory described what happened next, the D.A.

saw several people on the jury openly weeping. Would it be enough? The audience was horrified. All save for June, Gory's gal. She was stoic, sending him waves of support as he described how Axe had started at his feet and worked his way up. The enforcer had stopped at the femurs, leaving the shattered player's manhood intact, if that could be called a favor.

The cross-examination was brief. The defense wasn't counting on evidence or lack of. Their game was intimidation. The judge excused Gory from the box.

Gory turned his chair around and carefully wheeled down the ramp they'd built for him. His arms were still like Hercules's, but his crushed legs were nothing more than pudding wrapped in skin. He wouldn't let the doctors amputate, saying it would be better for his anger to see them every day.

❀ ❀ ❀

Out in the hallway, on recess, the prosecution's lead man felt like he'd been a tackling dummy for the Everett Eagles; hair mussed and head in his hands. June wheeled Gory over to him. His massive bulk wasn't easy to haul around yet, however, she never complained.

"We're not done yet," started Gory, "You'll be able to tear their alibis apart once they get up there."

The D.A. looked over at Gory, disputably the toughest player in the league for three years. As an attorney, he'd been the toughest, too. He'd taken on men like Big Papa as a lawyer and won. He didn't even have a witness like Gory, whose story was enough to break your heart. Yet, this trial was not going their way. Despite overwhelming amounts of evidence, he'd failed to convince the jury that bringing The Giordanos down was worth the risk to their own personal safety. He could see it in their eyes. They'd given up, and now he was starting to, as well.

"Take our friend down the hall for a coffee, Doll Face."

June nodded and pulled the attorney to his feet. She kept a hand on his shoulder as they walked. He looked back just in time to see an old Oriental man approach Gory. Gory shook the man's hand and in a voice fading as they moved farther away, the D.A. thought he heard him say, "Okay, now what was this you whispered to me in the courtroom about my legs?"

Now

"I've got to get home, Mr. Johnson."

"Pointer."

"Okay, Mr. Pointer. I've got to get home."

The kid was starting to annoy him. "Alright, Massey. I'm almost done here. How about you leave me the camera and I'll drop it off to be developed when I get back to the newspaper?"

The kid agreed and set the camera down on the bench next to the reporter. He skedaddled off as Pointer directed his last questions to the Eagles player.

The locker room emptied. Security was used to Pointer's face, sometimes asking him to turn off the lights before he left. Pointer used the facilities and looked at his notes as he trudged out. The soon-to-be ace reporter was beat. He'd been doing double duty for weeks trying to catch Gridiron in action. He'd been a day late and dollar short on two occasions, having chosen to stake out the wrong watering hole in Big Papa's empire. The masked madman had moved up from fronts to speakeasies. In one, he'd not only found illegal booze, but the deputy mayor, as well. This sent a ripple of fear through City Hall and now the police were hunting the man-monster too.

However, the creature was taking some damage. Last night, Pick and Axe had gotten him cornered and lobbed a grenade. No body was found afterwards, but bits of clothing and small traces of blood were. Apparently, Gridiron wasn't completely indestructible.

As Pointer walked to the parking lot, he heard a noise coming from the far end of the field. If he remembered right, that was where the team's old gym was. They'd upgraded the facilities with the increase in attendance. Gory's trial had brought the Eagles into the spotlight and now everyone wanted to watch football. It was "The Galloping Ghost" all over again.

The noise sounded like weights being lifted and dropped. Someone was still working out, even after a game. Pointer decided this would make a great side feature. "The Player Who Never Quit," he'd called it. It was odd that there was little light coming from the old building. The reporter could only see a flicker of a gas lamp through the window. Deciding that caution would be prudent, Pointer snuck up and peered in through the corner of the window.

Muscles rippled as nearly 300 pounds of weight rose and fell under the power of two massive arms. Even in the limited gaslight his skin shone metallic gray like the steel bumper of a pick-up truck, but unlike true steel, it rippled with the effort of the muscles underneath as it hefted its cargo. It was no body armor he wore. His body was the armor. Pointer could see the same effect on his chest and legs. He was glad he couldn't see the face, for the moment. He wanted to look without being discovered.

It would take more than metal skin to lift that much weight. He was strong beyond belief and those legs looked as if they could run, like a… a…

Why was Gridiron here, he thought, *at a football stadium? What was the connection?* Pointer got a fantastical idea. *It couldn't be. But it could. Could it?*

The clanging stopped and Pointer ducked down. There was rustling in the gym and the reporter hazarded another peek. Gridiron was getting dressed.

Pointer saw a mirror off to the side. If he angled it right, he'd be able to snap off a picture and capture Gridiron in all his glory. He crawled low past a few windows and peered up once more. The mirror was a floor length one and Pointer had him head to toe. He checked the camera for film, checked the flash and shot up quickly to snap the photograph. The movement caught Gridiron's eyes and he pulled the cloak up just as the flash went off. Pointer wasn't sure who was faster on the draw, but he wasn't waiting around to find out. He ran as if the devil himself was chasing him. The door to the gym slammed open, but Pointer had already gotten some distance. Thunderous footfalls sounded behind him as he beat feet to where his car was waiting. His was the only one left in the parking lot. Diving into the car, he tossed the camera on the passenger seat and dug for his keys. Gridiron cleared the stadium and was crossing the parking lot.

Where are my damn keys! Found them!

He cranked over the car once, then twice. Gridiron was less than two parking spaces away when it finally caught up. Pointer jammed down the gas and peeled rubber as the man-monster dove for his bumper. The car stopped. Pointer could feel the wheels spinning under him, but they were going nowhere. He looked in the rearview to see Gridiron lifting the back of the car by the bumper. The reporter swallowed and was about to just throw the camera out the window when the bumper gave way and the car screeched into motion. Fish-tailing around the parking lot until he got it back under control, Pointer thanked all that was holy for his luck. He made it to the newspaper without incident, but still called the police to watch over the building as he developed the picture. It wasn't perfect, it wasn't all of him, but it was enough. Pointer had gotten the first and only picture of the thing that called itself Gridiron, and now he knew why.

Two months ago

Gory wheeled himself next to the operating table. Dr. Phong Phat moved to help, but the former football player waved him away.

"That's fine. I can manage."

He grunted under the exertion of lifting his dead lower half out of the chair, but eventually got his backside firmly on the metal bench. After taking a moment to catch his breath, Gory then swung his useless legs up and laid back. Phong pushed the unnecessary chair away and began strapping Gory down. The linebacker tensed, remembering the last time he'd been strapped down.

Nervous for the first time since the crazy scientist approached him, Gory decided he needed to hear the whole thing one more time.

"Okay, Doc. Run me through this procedure again."

Phong tittered. "Oh, it very simple. I inject special serum in you of my own making. It like metal glue."

"Metal glue?" asked Gory, still not understanding the concept after the umpteenth time.

Phong moved to the head rest and tightened the head straps more, eliciting a grunt from his patient. "High in iron, it good for you. It go through your whole body.

Then, I stick needles in leg bones, like acupuncture. I stick one in every piece of bone in leg. Lots of needles."

Gory'd been stuck enough, so needles didn't bother him. The next part did.

"That's when you electrocute me?"

The Doctor tittered again, and Gory questioned the strange man's sanity, not for the first time. If it weren't for the chance to be healed, Gory would have told the little man to get lost weeks ago.

"Oh, I don't kill you. It just a low level current to attract serum to bone, make them all come together. Good as new, lickety-split."

The whole process would take two hours. There was no lickety-split about it.

"And you're sure this will work?"

Phong went about the task of sticking needles in Gory's legs. He put nearly fifty in his left foot alone.

"Absolutely! I fix my dog leg like he brand new. He like puppy again."

"Dog? You mean you've never tried this on a man before?"

The right foot done, Phong moved up the leg. "Oh, don't be big baby. Yes, you first man. I look in paper for long time to find man like you. You perfect specimen."

"Wait, Doc. I'm not so sure about this now. What about side effects?"

"Dog is fine."

"I'm not a dog!"

The right leg complete, the weird scientist set about the left. "All men are dog. You no worry. I come with money-back guarantee!"

Gory now understood why Phong had offered to do the procedure for free.

❉ ❉ ❉

"Mister Burrell? Mister Burrell? You wake now."

Gory's last thought before blacking out was that the herbs Phong had fed him were not helping with the pain like he said they would. It was even worse than the job Big Papa's goon thugs had done to him. The electricity raced through his whole body, not just his legs. It set every nerve on fire. He could smell his flesh burning and colors flashed like a merry-go-round beneath his clenched eye lids. The cure had been worse than the disease and then sweet bliss overtook him.

Gory had no idea how long he'd been out. It was morning when they started, but as he opened his eyes slowly, he could see street lamps out the window. He was still at the lab, but in a soft bed. How the micro Asian man had gotten him to it, he didn't want to know. What he needed to know was, had it been worth it?

Gory got to his elbows and looked down at his legs. His toes pointed up under the sheet. He wiggled them then rotated his feet. Everything felt good. No pain. No crunching of bone against bone. He pulled his knees up to his chest slowly. They were stiff, but movable. Flipping back the sheet, he swung his legs over the side. He pushed off from the bed and wobbled, the first time he'd been on his walking sticks in months.

"Oh, it very simple. I inject special serum in you of my own making. It like metal glue."

"Whoa, big man. Take it easy. You no walk in long time. Need to learn again."

Gory smirked. "The only thing I need to learn now if how soon I can start playing football!"

"No, not that simple." Phong shook his head. "You have metal bones now. You play game and you hurt people you hit. Not like before. You break them in two."

Gory hadn't considered that. He couldn't play football anymore. He sat back down to think about the revelation. What did that mean? Who was he now?

It didn't take long before he saw June and April in his mind. He was to be a husband and a father. That's what was important! He could push April on the swing set at the park. He could make love to his wife on their honeymoon. He could find a job somewhere that needed a guy with bones of steel. He'd make it work!

Gory jumped up elated at his new found peace, but over compensated for the new strength in his legs. He flew forward and put his hands out to grab a hold of something. One of the lab tables was near him and he reached for it. Phong yelled, "NO! Not that table!" but it was too late. Gory hit the edge of it, flipping all its contents into the air. A large beaker had been perched at the opposite end. It went up and its liquid contents sloshed over Gory's body. The strange substance went everywhere else. It crawled over his skin until every inch of him felt wet. Then as quickly as it coated him, it dried, hardening fast and making him feel like a statue.

"Nonono!" stammered Phong. "This no good! You turn into sculpture. I must fix." Gory heard a sound like the one when Phong turned on his electro-magnetometer to electrocute Gory earlier that morning. He could feel the air become ionized as it did before starting during the procedure. He wanted to scream for the doctor to stop, but it was too late. Needles jabbed into his skin and the electricity coursed through him once again, and with it, returned the pain.

Now

June was running late. She entered through the service entrance and made her way to clock in. No sooner had she when riotous noise reached her ears. There was a party going on in the bullpen. Not sure if she should poke her head in or not, hoping not to attract attention to her tardiness, nosiness won out and she slipped in behind the cavalcade of writer's, editors and photographers. A champagne bottle popped and a cheer arose. Looking through the throng, June spotted Terry in the center of the hullabaloo. He stood on a desk with the Chief and was swigging down some of the bubbly. People patted his leg in a show of support.

"To the newest star reporter at the Everett Herald; Terry "Pointer" Johnston! Take a bow, Pointer!"

Terry bowed at the waist and as he came up, he saw June in the back of the crowd. Their eyes locked for a moment, and then Terry looked away quickly, an embarrassment showing on his face. June was surprised he didn't come running to her, sweeping her into his winner's circle. What was going on?

She leaned over to the closest person to her, "What's this all about? I just got here."

A crossword editor, the type to be relegated to the back of a crowd such as this, grinned a Cheshire Cat's grin, happy to be in the know for once and not the last one at that. "Pointer got a photo of Gridiron. Not just a fleeting one, but a full on, clear as day, snap-shot! He said it nearly cost him his life."

June noticed the editor was clutching the morning edition. She asked if she could look, and the man reluctantly handed over his prize. And there it was, headlines screaming "Monster Caught on Film!"

It was a reversed image, the edge of a mirror clearly seen. She looked at the creature, a majority of it covered in clothing and a mask, but the eyes were uncovered. She stared at the eyes. They were angry, yet she thought they were also scared. She knew those eyes. She looked into them a hundred times, a thousand. She knew who they belonged to. The paper fell from her hands as she ran from the room; tears dropping like rain behind her.

❄ ❄ ❄

Pointer knocked at June's door. She knew it was him. He would have heard by now; her running out of the building a weepy mess. He would be the only one to come check on her. Anyone else would have just thought her a scared little rabbit. But Terry would know. He'd have to come to her eventually, if he was any sort of a man.

She opened the door and stood there, morning edition held in front of her like a police officers badge. "How long have you known?"

He held his head down in shame. "I didn't. Not for sure. Things that didn't add up at first, but it made sense when you looked at it like a reporter."

June didn't let him cross her threshold yet. "But you knew when you saw him. When you took the photo. When you pasted it on the front page."

The reporter kept his head low.

"How could you? How could you do this without talking to me? Was your precious position with the paper that important? That you'd risk everyone finding out?"

Terry finally looked up, "But I didn't, did I? Nowhere in that article does it give his name. I left it deliberately vague." He grabbed the paper from her and pointed to a line. He read it from memory, "'The man that calls himself Gridiron was spotted in an undisclosed location as he prepared to visit more mayhem on evildoers in the city.' I could have said more. I know so much more. But I didn't."

"What do you know? What's going on?" June was frantic now. Emotions on overdrive, she pushed at Pointer, demanding him to tell all his secrets. "Where is he hiding? Why is he doing this? How did he become this... this..."

"Monster?"

The tears started again and Pointer drew her in for a hug. It wasn't the hug of a suitor, but a friend. She needed it and let lose her anguish. When the sobbing stopped, they sat on the couch. He filled June in on all that he knew.

"I think there's still a good man under all that metal," reasoned Pointer, "He hasn't hurt any innocent bystanders yet. He chooses his targets carefully; always Big Papa's enterprises. He's dismantling The Giordanos one piece at a time. He's doing what the courts couldn't."

"Big Papa nearly killed him once. They're going to keep at it until he is hurt, or someone else gets hurt accidentally. He's got to stop. I don't care if he's metal, as long as he's alive."

His bloodhound nose could see where this was going, "Now, listen, June. You can't go after him. I doubt he'll be at the gym anymore now that I've seen him there. He'll go deeper into hiding, or worse, rush his end game."

June was puzzled, "What end game?"

Pointer stood up and paced around. "No one's gotten close to him. Not until recently. He's either getting tired, or impatient. Either way, he's sloppy. First the grenade that injured him, now the front page. Police will now be on the look-out for him and Big Papa knows he can be hurt. He's running out of time to take The Giordanos down."

"So you think he'll do something stupid?"

"I think he'll take the fight to Big Papa. He looked healed, so that could be any time."

June shot up, "I've got to stop him. They'll kill him, Pointer."

His face lit up. "You called me Pointer."

June hadn't realized her slip. "You're an ace reporter now. I have to get used to that. Now, you're going to help me get into Big Papa's restaurant."

He held his hands up to stop her. "No way! Not in a billion years."

She set her jaw and advanced on him. "I'm going with or without you, but if you help me get a job there, then you'll have the inside track on Big Papa and anything that goes down."

"You're crazy! Pick and Axe will recognize you from the trial."

Twirling, June laughed, "I'll just have to disguise myself. A wig and some new clothes ought to do it. Plus, if I can find out how they plan to stop Gordon—"

"Gridiron," Pointer corrected, "You can never use his name or they'll know who he is, if they haven't figured it out already."

"If they had, I doubt I'd still be here. But you're right. If I can find out what they plan to do to Gridiron, then I can tell you and you can warn him."

"That's assuming a lot, Toots."

She headed for the bedroom, "I think I still have a wig from Halloween." She disappeared behind a door, but continued to call out, "And yes, it is. But it's better than sitting around waiting to read your story about the death of Gridiron."

Pointer was left wondering who was crazier; Gridiron or his girlfriend?

One Month Ago

Gory stumbled through the dark alleyway, a moth-eaten blanket covering his immense frame. He was a modern day Quasimodo; a man with no home, reprehensible to gaze upon, his insides a turmoil of anger and sadness, depression and loneliness. Nothing Phong did could reverse the process and only caused more pain. He should be grateful his organs hadn't turned to metal as well. The former football player was tired; the weight of his skin only held upright by his metal bones. And it hurt, the metal pulling against the flesh of his muscles, like a million demons scratching at him constantly.

He needed somewhere to hide, somewhere where no one would find him. He couldn't go to June's, not like this. He hadn't made friends on the team that he could trust. He only had himself.

Instinct took him towards the edge of town, to the football stadium. He remembered the old shed, the one where they used to train before the new workout area was added to the locker room. There were cots, and clothes, and no one used it in the off season. He could hide there for a month and be gone before the team started anew.

The lock was easy to bust with his new strength. He rumbled around in the dark until he found a flashlight. The torch revealed a dust covered room with weight benches. He picked one strong enough to hold his massive bulk and laid down his world weary head. The blanket wouldn't warm his metal skeleton, but he wrapped himself in it, anyway. Tomorrow he'd figure things out. Tomorrow he'd start planning his revenge.

❀ ❀ ❀

He slept most of the day and kept hidden until dark. He went out again to gather food. Once satiated, he considered a disguise to work the voodoo he was planning.

Big Papa had taken everything away from him; his job, his love, his soon-to-be step-daughter. They were all out of his reach. Now, Gory would start taking things away from Big Papa. He'd start small by rattling the chains of the small fries, like when he smack-talked an opposing team. Gory found the weakest players and browbeat them, creating rumors about his merciless play. After that, he'd hunt the front line; the guys between him and his goal: the quarterback. Once they were scared, he'd start getting in the mind of their leader. He'd make mistakes, fumble plays, chose the wrong guys to commit to defense. He'd tear apart Big Papa's team, as he'd done so many others in the past.

He rooted around the lockers finding old pads that he could rework for his bulk. There were big players on the team, so Gory looked for some of their leftover shirts and pants. He couldn't be too obvious about the design. If he looked too much like a football player that might bring Big Papa down on the team, but he could modify what he found to imply the same toughness and intimidation he brought to the field.

Finally, needing a mask to cover his face, he looked around in the storage shed. Some joker had brought in a clown mask and stuck it on a tackling dummy. It had creeped everyone out and made them want to hit the dummy harder. It was still there, so he cut out the smile and glued it onto a torn piece of cloth. After wrapping it over his nose and chin, only his eyes remained uncovered, so that he'd have the best angle of vision. Once dressed, he looked at himself in the mirror. The effect was chilling. Anyone who saw him would be terrified. They'd talk about him until Big Papa himself was wetting his expensive suits.

But what would they call him? Gordon "Gory" Burrell was gone, as far as anyone was concerned. He needed a new name. One that would send chills up the collective spine of The Giordanos.

On the wall was a framed newspaper sports page article. It was twenty years old, yellowed and faded, but he could still make out the headline:

Roosevelt Visits Gridiron Board

Gory's smile mimicked the **fake** one he wore. He knew who he was to be from that point forward. He pulled up the hood and went to find his first target.

Now

Big Papa was nervous and when Big Papa was nervous, Big Papa ate. Some say he built his empire so big hoping he'd never have to worry again, but the more he amassed, the more he worried and the more he ate, until Big Papa's girth was as big as his holdings. His momma said he was a worrier, but she was always critical of him. If he didn't worry, she'd say he wasn't worried enough.

Instead, he put people around him to solve his problems, so he wouldn't worry so much. Pick and Axe were his most trusted enforcers and they still couldn't solve his latest concern.

"You goombas are worthless!" It was the first time Big Papa had to reprimand the pair. They took it in stride, their own work ethic making them feel low enough already. "I can't get you to do one simple thing; blot out one man. Sure he's made of metal, but you two were supposed to have brass knockers bigger than anyone's. How could you do this to me?"

They said nothing. The grenade should have worked. They found blood in the wreckage, but not enough to confirm a kill. Then the blab sheet ran that picture and they knew for sure they'd failed. Axe was taking it the hardest as it had been a grenade his father had brought back from Germany and was told to use only in case of emergency. He stood there now, seething inside, thinking of how disappointed his father would have been and how much worse the tongue lashing would have been in comparison to Big Papa's.

Pick, on the other hand, was considering if it was time to join his aunt in the floral delivery business.

Big Papa continued, oblivious to their thoughts, "So I'm getting you a little help."

With a snap of his fingers, a man entered through the alcove wheeling a cart with a tablecloth over it. Young and dressed in army fatigues, He paused before the large man and saluted. Big Papa laughed with merriment, the first either of his enforcers had heard in months. "Come here, you wise guy, and give your uncle a hug!"

Seriousness gone, the soldier bent over for the offered affections, returning them in kind. After, the Patriarch introduced the grunt, "This is my nephew Vito, Charley's brother. Vito got the good looks and the brains of the family. These are the boys, Vito. Say Hi."

Vito shook the enforcers' hands in turn. He made no move to acknowledge his brother who hovered behind their uncle. "Good. Now Vito here did something I thought was stupid last year, but in hindsight, it was most fortuitous. He went against our wishes and joined the army."

"After all the stories I heard about the war, I felt in my *patriotic duty* to serve." Vito beamed with pride. His Uncle did likewise.

"You hear that? Patriotic Duty. We told him that he could do that as a member of the Giordanos, as we are a very patriotic family, aren't we?"

The enforcers agreed, but kept eyeing the shapes under the cloth.

"So, when you two yahoos couldn't get the job done, I starts thinking; who is the best killer I know? And then I remember Vito here. Not only is he a member of family, but he's been trained by our own government to kill anything. Ain't that right, Vito."

"That's right, Uncle."

Big Papa laughed. "I love this kid so much, he's the only one I let call me Uncle." Even Big Papa's momma called him Big Papa these days. "So, why don't you show the boys what Uncle Sam has created for us?"

"Sure thing, Uncle." Vito pulled back the cloth revealing three weapons, each more impressive than the first. "Okay, for starters we have the M1918A2, or BAR for short." The grunt hoisted the rifle which had its own bipod at the end of the barrel. "This baby is a semi-automatic that will punch a hole in a wall you could put your fist through. It's a little bulky and not easily carried, thus the stand at the end, but if you have time to set it up, this should give your metal man something to think about."

Axe reached for the gun and had no problem holding it in a firing position. Impressed Vito complimented, "Or, if you're Axe here, you pop it like a hand-gun! Ha!"

Next, he hoisted the second gun, this twice the size of the first. It had a flat end and legs in the center of the gun. "This is your standard issue anti-tank Browning M2 machine gun. We used this beauty to punch holes in the Huns' A7V tanks. They hated it when one of these bullets bounced around inside their cabin. Tore the crap out of them."

"Hey, watch the language. There are women present."

Big Papa motioned towards a waitress that was bringing him a huge plate of pasta. She was young with black hair, beautiful eyes and hourglass figure. Exactly the type Big Papa preferred bringing him his repast.

Vito bowed. "Sorry, Miss."

She smiled and said with a clearly New Jersey accent, "It's nothing I ain't hoird before." She curtsied on her way out.

Big Papa was amused. "I like that dame!"

All the guys laughed, save for Pick who studied the broad as she left. There was something familiar about her, but he couldn't quite place it.

The last thing Vito showed them looked like a stovepipe with a gun grip.

"Now this thing is what you'd call experimental. This guy I know, Eddie, was trying to design something to shoot an M10 grenade. He got tired of having to run up to a tank and throw it."

"Yeah, I can see where that'd be a problem," said Big Papa.

"Yeah, so he's been toying around with some different designs. He's got this one to work pretty well, but it only works once, then you got to get rid of it. Oh, and you can't stand behind it."

Pick was curious, "What happens if you stand behind it?"

Vito made a whooshing sound and with his hands made a big explosion. "Ba-da-boom!"

Pick nodded appreciatively. "I'll keep that in mind."

Axe set down the other guns and grenade launcher. "What's he call it?"

"A bazooka. Cause that's what you yell when you see those krauts go up! BAZOOKA!"

They all had a good laugh and Vito turned to Big Papa to say goodbye. "I'll need those back soon, okay, Uncle?"

"As soon as we make shrapnel of this metal man. Shouldn't take long now that they boys here have some sting. Capiche?"

"Capiche!"

❊ ❊ ❊

June finished her table orders and snuck back to where she knew there was a phone. She adjusted the wig because it cut into her head. She didn't know how actresses did it. Quickly dialing the squawk-box, she hoped Pointer was waiting right by his end, as promised. It rang once... twice...

"June?"

"Yeah, it's me. I don't have long. The one they call Pick was eyeing me funny."

"Get out of there!"

"I will, but first, listen. They have guns, Pointer. Big ones. Ones that'll hurt him, even through his met—"

Pick had slipped up behind June and wrapped a hand over her mouth. She tried to scream, but his grip was too tight. He coiled himself around her, so she couldn't break free. Pointer, realizing something was wrong, yelled into the receiver.

"June! June! What's going on?"

Pick pushed June into Axe's waiting arms. In the moment she had her mouth free she cried, "It's a trap!"

Pick put the phone to his face, "You're that reporter aren't you? Well, here's a scoop for you. Thanks to this little lady, we now know who Gridiron is, as I'm sure you do, too. So, you go find that freak of nature so we can finish the job we started, understand?"

"If you harm her…"

"This little number? Not a chance. Not until after her fiancé comes to rescue her and we break him into ball bearings. Then we'll decide what to do with her. You, on the other hand, have bigger problems. You need to find that abomination and tell him to meet us at Eagle Stadium."

Resigned to the hand fate dealt, Pointer hung up.

❀ ❀ ❀

Not sure where to start looking, Pointer drove around for hours hoping to catch a glimpse of Gridiron leaping across roof tops or skulking down alleys. Finally, with no recourse left, he headed toward the stadium. While the reporter sat at a red light, he noticed the streets were deserted of cars and pedestrian traffic. This wasn't odd, being the time of night it was, but it did explain why Gridiron had chosen that moment to yank open his door and drag Pointer into the night.

"Gory! Wait!"

As an answer, Pointer was thrown across the dark alley. He hit several trash cans, knocking them over. Above the rattling, he could hear Gridiron's growl.

"Gory is dead."

Pointer wasted no time in scrambling to his feet. "We need to talk!" He was pushed again, stumbled backwards, slipped on some discarded food and landed flat on his back.

"The only reason you're alive is because you didn't print my name in your story. What do you want next? An interview?"

The reporter got onto all fours and moved away from the voice. He'd heard Gory before a big game; the desire to break the other team. Gridiron was like that, only ten times worse.

"It's about June!"

Gridiron lifted Pointer up off the ground by his jacket and suspended him in air.

"Oh, let me guess? Your carelessness with the photo? Did someone piece it together? Is she in danger?"

Hot breath blew in Pointer's face. He didn't want to say what he had to, but it a half-sob he croaked, "She figured it out."

"And she's heartbroken now? Now that she knows what a monster I've become? Didn't you think about that before you printed the photo? Was fame worth all that?

Your precious position?"

With each question, Gridiron shook the reporter making the words strike home even harder. Pointer realized he traded June for a premium spot in the bullpen. He thought it'd all work out in the end, but it hadn't and now…

"She's in danger! And it's all my fault!"

Gridiron dropped him and Pointer sat disgusted by his own actions. He was ready for the former football to snap his neck and be done with it. What he wasn't prepared for was Gridiron's words.

"No, it's not your fault. It's mine."

"Huh?"

Gridiron sat down on some boxes under a back door light. He was weary to the eye, like a statue left in the elements for too long; the anger was rusting him from the inside.

"I did this to myself. I believed I was less of a man without my legs. I convinced myself I would be a horrible husband and father. So, I tried to defy nature and wound up a freak. By then my rage was so strong I needed to direct it at someone. I couldn't direct it at me, so I took on Big Papa. Like that'd make a difference."

"Big Papa! That's right! Big Papa's men have got June!"

"WHAT!"

Gridiron loomed over Pointer, making the reporter feel like he might kill him after all. "June wanted to help you so she snuck into Big Papa's restaurant. She found out they've got big guns to use against you, but they spotted her and figured out who you are, were, whatever! They're going to kill her if you don't walk into their trap!"

All the anger came rushing back. The pain was tolerable as long as she was okay, but June in danger made the rage stronger than ever. Fire burned in his soul and Big Papa would be sacked tonight.

❊ ❊ ❊

June hung from the goal post. They had bound her hands and looped the rope over the uprights. Her legs swung free and her right shoe had dropped the few inches to the ground. Somehow, the left one stayed on.

She couldn't see them, but she knew where the enforcers lay in wait. Axe was sprawled down on the ground in the hallway leading to the visitor's locker room. The BAR lined up on her. He'd get Gridiron or her or both of them with the shot.

Pick was hiding in the announcer's booth with the anti-tank gun. Big Papa had wanted to send more men, but these two had called it a matter of honor. If they didn't bring back something to hang on Big Papa's wall, then they'd rather be dead. Big Papa looked pleased when they said it, but then kept the bazooka in case they failed.

They'd turned on all the overhead lights, as if a night game was being played. June knew that this was no game and two people would most likely be dead tonight. Maybe only one, if Pointer couldn't find Gridiron. She feared for April, mostly, not for herself. To lose one parent was tough enough, then Gordon. But if she lost her mom, April would withdraw from life where no one could reach her.

A shape passed by one the entrances to the stadium. Someone was here. A projectile launched from the shadows flew straight and clear into one of the large stadium lights. It went out with a bang and crinkle of glass. A ball dropped to the field and June knew Gridiron had arrived.

Another light followed the first. And another. Finally, a noise came over the loudspeaker. It was Pick. "That's enough, Gory, lest we start punching holes through your little lady friend here. Now, good and slow, I want you to walk out into the center of the field."

The shape she'd seen stepped out of the shadows and moved toward midfield. He was big, but not as giant as he'd been portrayed. His football uniform was barely visible under a large trench coat and his face hidden behind that hideous smile. When she'd seen the photo, she had really focused only on the eyes and not the rest of him. But seeing him now as he approached, she could see that he'd really changed. Even his walk was different.

The man-mountain stopped at the fifty yard line. Pick continued with the directions, "Now please remove that mask and coat. We want to have a good look at you."

From the angle he stood, they couldn't see what she saw. June gasped. It wasn't Gordon behind the mask. It was Pointer.

He dropped the trench and mask in one fluid movement and yelled, "Now!"

All the lights went out. Gridiron must have cut the power. Moonlight filled the arena and June watched as Pointer ran in full football gear, firing a gun towards the darkened hallway where Axe was. Flashes of light sparked in return and the cacophony of gunfire filled the air. Pointer got hit in the leg, causing him to go into a diving roll, but it must have just grazed him for he kept his forward momentum towards her. If he was here to rescue her, then where was Gridiron?

❖ ❖ ❖

Pick knew the day he dropped the toothpick from his lips was the day he died. He was starting to believe that might be today. While Axe was firing at the decoy, Pick scanned the entrances hoping to spot movement. He only needed one shot. If he could get it off, his chances of surviving this night increased.

The gun was too heavy to carry alone, but he could slide it across the table in the booth. He angled it back and forth, trying to see both ends of the stadium at the same time. There was a loud thump, like something had landed in the bleachers.

WHUMP! WHUMP! WHUMP!

Gridiron was in the stands and approaching at high speed. Pick could see the shape barely, but enough to move the gun into position. He waited until the monster was closer. He could almost make out the face, the teeth glistening in the starshine. He had him. He had him dead to rights. He squeezed the trigger and gunfire blossomed, sending its projectile right into the spot where Gridiron stood.

Had stood.

Pick looked up and saw the descending form in the light of the moon. Gridiron smashed through the roof and landed feet away from Pick. The hit man fell backwards, trying to take the gun with him. If he could just swing it around, but Gridiron was too fast. He grabbed the barrel and bent it up, making it useless to fire. A snarl escaped his lips and Pick was sure he'd never seen another being that filled with rage before in his life.

Scrambling backwards out the door, Pick raced across and down the stands. The thudding followed and Pick knew Gridiron was right behind him. He lost his footing and tumbled down a dozen rows to land upright against the bottom railing. The mouthpiece of the mob turned just as Gridiron reached him, the full force of his tackle taking them through the railing and down onto the field. Pick was trapped under the metal gargantuan and heard every bone in his body break even before he felt it. Pain took him into unconsciousness, the toothpick dropping to the ground beside him.

❀ ❀ ❀

The pain in Pointer's leg was less than he imagined being shot felt like, whether it was due to being grazed, or the thickness of the pads Gridiron had dressed him in. They might have overdone it, as it was hard to run in all that gear. However, he could move and he could get to June. The problem was that when he got there, though, they'd both be sitting ducks. He fired towards the visitor's locker room again knowing it wasn't doing diddly except give the maniac with the sniper rifle something to shoot at. Pointer had to change tactics.

He changed direction away from June. Still firing, he was pleased when the muscle kept focused on him. Did he just think that? Pointer was now as crazy as the rest of them.

Axe had left the shelter of the alcove and now walked along the sidelines firing the mammoth gun with both hands. If Pointer was any slower, he'd be Swiss cheese by now. Their eyes were adjusting to the low light and things became clearer. The reporter spotted something on the sidelines and made a break for it. Laughing as he tried to gun the fleeing man down, Axe seemed to have an endless supply of ammunition. Reaching his goal, Pointer dived behind the tackling dummies. Holes were punched through them by the large caliber bullets, but it gave him a sense of shielding, however unreliable it was. The dummies were on wheels and keeping his head down, Pointer pushed with all his strength to get them rolling. He heard Axe start in surprise and the laughter stopped. As Pointer got closer, he risked a peek only to see Axe back-pedaling.

So focused was Axe on Pointer's approach, he didn't see what had come up behind him. The hit man smashed into the metal monument that was Gridiron. He spun, but the gun was torn from his hands and tossed away.

The thudding followed and Pick knew Gridiron was right behind him.

"Mer-cy!" Axe croaked, as a metal gauntlet wrapped around his throat.

Gridiron laughed through gritted teeth, "Listen to him, would ya, Pointer? 'Mercy,' he says!"

"Yeah, Gory, I heard him," Pointer echoed as he approached.

"What mercy did you show me when you took a sledgehammer to my legs? What mercy have you ever shown any of your victims?"

"Gordon 'Gory' Burrell! You put that man down right this instant!"

Gridiron and Pointer turned to see that the dangling June was furious. She motioned with her face for them to look down. Gridiron realized he was holding Axe about six inches off the ground.

"This doesn't concern you, June!"

"Like blazes, it doesn't! Down! Now!"

Pointer reached into the waistband of Axe's suit and retrieved a handgun. He nodded to Gridiron who let the thug drop.

"They must be stopped, June or you and April will never be safe."

He moved to free his fiancé, snapping the ropes with one hand, while holding her in his other arm. June focused on him, eyes piercing his soul. "And what would I tell April? That the man she loves like a father was no better than the men he's out there trying to protect her from? No. Pointer has the whole city believing you're some sort of hero."

She melted into him, wrapping her arms around his neck and whispering to him in a soft voice, "Be one."

It didn't come easy, but he found the strength to put his arms around her and complete their embrace. After a few moments, he had to push her away, his face darkening into something unreadable.

"It has to end tonight."

He set her down and walked over to the discarded the mask and coat. June watched as the man she loved donned his persona once more. When he faced her he said, "Gordon is dead, but the man he once was is not. I am Gridiron and I will protect you."

❁ ❁ ❁

Big Papa was too nervous to even eat. It was the first time Charlie had ever seen him not eat. They both knew whoever walked through that door was going to decide the fate of The Giordanos. Charlie wasn't stupid. He knew that if Big Papa went down, then he went, too. He'd turn state's evidence and get a reduced sentence, but Charlie wasn't the type to do well in jail. He was smarter than anyone expected, playing the fool to make him appear harmless. As long as his brother served in the army, Charlie was the only direct heir to business, and he knew the business backwards and forwards.

It was Charlie that had suggested to Big Papa that Gordon Burrell might be approachable to take a dive, knowing full well he wouldn't. It has been Charlie that suggested to Axe that kneecapping the football player would be a fitting punishment. It was Charlie who'd contacted Phong, a scientist in the Asian cartels' employ and brought him to America to meet with Gory. It had been Charlie that whispered to his Uncle that Vito might have weapons they could use on Gridiron. And, ultimately, it would be Charlie who walked away from all of this unscathed.

"Charlie! Come here you miserable excuse for a lackey!"

"Yes, Big Papa?"

"This started with you and that tip, so I've decided it'll be you that finishes it."

Charlie frowned, but inside, it was exactly what he expected the fat tub of lard to do. "What do you want me to do, Big Papa?"

"I want you to take that bazooka thing and get ready to blow a hole in anything that comes through that door that's not Pick or Axe. Capiche?"

Charlie loudly swallowed to imply nervousness, but felt the rush of his plan reaching fruition. "Yes, Big Papa."

He took the bazooka and hefted it to his shoulder.

"Now remember! Watch where you point the back of that thing. I don't want to get my hair singed off."

Oh, thought Charlie, I know right where to point it.

The restaurant's back room was secluded from prying eyes, but Big Papa had a two way mirror to spy on the main dining area. Charlie waited. Gridiron would make a big entrance. He picked the right guy to orchestrate Big Papa's downfall. No subtly at all. The throng of people feasted on the best pasta in the city, many of them knowing fully well who owned the place. They'd visited Big Papa's gin joints and knew where the power flowed from. That power would be his soon.

The doors flung open and there Gridiron stood. The lighting in the establishment was set on moody, but it just made the monster all the more nightmarish. Flickering candles played off his dark iron hide and gave the impression of a fire burning under the surface. The man-mountain muttered a single "GO!" and the people scattered past him like rats fleeing the Titanic. Charlie situated the bazooka on his shoulder and took aim at the advancing figure. He was too big to miss, and he'd never dodge something he didn't see coming. Charlie couldn't wait much longer, there were going to be casualties either way, but Big Papa would get the blame when they found the bazooka in his dead hands.

"Charlie! What are you? Deaf as well as dumb? I told you watch where you point the backend of that thing!"

The nephew gave his Patriarch a quick sideways glance and said, "I'm neither, Uncle" and pulled the trigger. Flames erupted from either end of the bazooka, engulfing the Mob Boss's head in a blazing mushroom cloud in the back and sending the rocket propelled grenade out the front. It blasted through the window and would have struck home, but Gridiron dropped hands first to the ground. The missile passed over him and continued through the front window. It embedded into a car outside and destroyed it in a magnificent light show of sound and noise. Shrapnel sprayed the escaping crowd and many were knocked over in the concussion.

Charlie realized someone must have lived to tell Gridiron about the weapon. All he'd have to do is listen for the ignition and hit the dirt. It was a flaw, but not a fatal one. He still propped the bazooka in Big Papa's dead hand and vamoosed through the kitchen exit.

There would be confusion and chaos. Even if the cops did their jobs, Charlie would derail the investigation using the mob's money. Once the transition of power was complete, he'd deal with that lucky bastard Gordon Burrell.

Charlie had left his car by the back door. He slid in behind the seat and gunned the engine. Sticking the car in first, he applied pressure to the pedal but the car didn't move. He pressed harder and could hear the squeal of tires on asphalt, but there was still no movement. When the car's back end lifted up, Charlie knew what was happening. He grabbed a gun from the glove box and shot through his back window. The bullets bounced off Gridiron's flesh as if they were BBs.

"Hey, Charlie," Gridiron spoke, "Nobody ever asks me what I did before pro-football. In all those interviews, they only wanted to know about Gory the gridiron beast. No one asked about Gordon. You know what I did?"

Charlie kept the pedal floored, hoping that Gridiron would get tired of yapping and drop him. "No. What did you do before you became a freak of nature?"

In the rear-view mirror, the former football player, now guardian of the city, held something up in his free hand. It looked like a brake pedal. "I was a mechanic."

The car dropped and lurched forward. Charlie was pinned to the back of his seat, and could only be a passenger on his car's trajectory. It leapt from the alley and plowed directly into the wall across the street. The car made a sickening sound and it accordioned, flames shooting from the engine as fuel ignited. There was a small explosion and with it, the Giordanos died.

❈ ❈ ❈

Pointer was busy over the next several weeks. The Chief put him in charge of organizing the teams of reporters covering "The Fall of The Mob," as the headlines screamed. There was already talk of a promotion to Assistant Chief, but the reporter repeatedly said that after the mess was over, and his leg had time to heal, his was going back on the beat where he felt like he belonged.

But while Pointer was still on point, there were interviews to gather; from every two-bit thug in Everett to anti-racketeering Feds in Washington. Pick and Axe were both going to jail this time, no savior in sight, and that trial would need to be covered. Pointer found it pleasingly ironic that Pick would be testifying from a wheelchair. Rumors had Vito Giordano going AWOL after an inquiry into some stolen weapons was started by the military. No one knew where he was, but June was sure he was up to no good.

The rush wouldn't last long, as bad things were brewing overseas. War was in the air and that meant jobs for the people of America. They'd be focused on the future soon, not on a past filled with mobsters and monsters.

June sat on the rooftop with her daughter April. Their apartment building had a nice view of Everett up there and since the events of the last few weeks were winding down, she'd taken to coming up here with April to enjoy the last of summer.

"You know what tomorrow is?"

April's faced beamed, "Football season starts!"

"Yes, my baby girl. Why don't we go root the Eagles on to a victory?"

The young girl jumped up and down with joy and hugged her mom. June didn't let go right away, looking over the blonde curls into the city. He was out there, somewhere. Gridiron left her a note saying he made no apologies for how things turned out, but because of it, wouldn't be returning any time soon. He wanted the hoopla to die down and people to ever forget Gory ever existed.

Like that will happen, she thought. No, Gordon. You left your mark on Everett; as a man, as a player and as a hero. It is yours to love and protect, just as we love you.

June took her daughter back inside, turning just a moment too soon to see the metal guardian three buildings over return to his job as sentinel over the city.

THE END

A Football Hero

by David Boop

Gridiron came about as a way for Airship 27 head honcho Ron Fortier to shut me up.

Let me explain. I'd wanted to work with A27 for almost a year, ever since Ron reviewed my novel and told me all about the group. I looked into writing for one of the many pulp heroes they "represent," but couldn't find the right fit. I also spent time whining to Ron that my novel, set in 1953, wasn't eligible for the Pulp Factory Awards. Ron, ever the patient man, listened and then said, "Why not create your own pulp hero?"

Why not, indeed! As long as it was set in the 30's and embodied all that we know and love about pulps, then Ron would take a look at it.

Now the question was what concept would I base my character on?

I spent some time researching the 30's and stumbled across some interesting facts about football during that era. It was new and considered kind of a joke by many. Sure, they played it in college, but football wasn't anything anyone would pay to see, right? But that all changed with Red Grange, the Galloping Ghost. He was so popular that he single handedly saved a franchise team via ticket sales alone. It's he who gave the fledgling National Football League its legitimacy. Red once ran for 252 yards and scored four touchdowns in the first 12 minutes of a game. There's a hero! I knew my guy would have to have that same level of dedication.

I created Gordon "Gory" Burrell to be a defensive player instead of offensive because eventually he would be a defender of not only an end zone, but of a whole city. I also wanted his girlfriend to have a child for future story potential. Knowing what was going to happen to his body, children would be, er, difficult.

The villains would be the mob, as they were most likely to be involved in sports. However, to make them less two-dimensional, I layered the story with levels of intrigue. The funny thing is, making Gridiron more cajones than cabeza, he all but ignores the subtext. Point him at a target and let him go! The twists are for us the readers, not him.

Pick and Axe were fun to write as enforcers. I wanted the classic odd hit men and flavored them to be just strange enough to be a threat while providing a touch of comic relief. Additionally, the character of Pointer was going to be more comical, but my writers group pushed me to make him a serious reporter. They were right.

Finally, I broke two rules of short story writing; multiple POVs and flashbacks. I did the first because it was important for us, as the readers, to see the effect Gridiron was having on the different players in the story without having to be dialog intensive. By doing an ascending flashback, I allowed myself a level of interaction between timelines I'd never experienced before. Plus, it gets us into the action quicker. By the story's acceptance into this volume, I believe that it worked, but I'll let you be the judge. Enjoy!

DAVID BOOP - a Denver-based author is a single dad, returning college student and full-time mailroom supervisor. He's done jobs as diverse as DJ, film critic and Beetlejuice impersonator. As a journalist, he covered the Columbine Massacre. His first novel was the sci-fi noir *She Murdered Me with Science.* He's had over a dozen short stories appear in magazines and anthologies. Born in CT, he keeps moving farther west as he gets older. Stops have included WI, TN, CO, and AZ. General interests include noir and sci-fi films, theater, stand-up comedy and The Blues. Find out more on FaceBook or at www.davidboop.com.

Dusk
The Sacred and the Profane

by Barry Reese

Chapter I.
The Dead Man's Skull

February 1933 – Atlanta, Georgia

Benny Lancaster felt like his heart was about to explode. It was hammering painfully hard in his chest and as he rounded the corner and found himself facing the dead end of an alleyway, he muttered a string of curses that would have made a sailor wince in surprise. He leaned against the wall and steadied himself, reaching into the pockets of his coat so he could reassure himself that his treasures were still there. One of them, his pistol, he pulled out into the open. There were still one bullet in the chamber and he'd have to make it count – or else he'd end up just like Big Al and Kenny. They were lying in pools of their own blood a few blocks back.

The other prize that he carried was left in its pocket, the weight of it causing his coat to lean heavily to the left. Benny knew how valuable it was but he refused to think about it too much – it unnerved him. He heard footsteps coming towards the alleyway and he raised his gun, prepared to fire the moment she came into view. He'd heard stories that bullets didn't faze her but he refused to believe that. She was as human as he was – she had to be.

The footsteps came to a halt and the seconds began to stretch into moments. Benny swallowed hard, wondering what the hell she was up to. His hand was beginning to shake under the strain and he began looking around quickly. There was a small grating nearby and he could hear the rush of water from below. It was a storm sewer and Benny suddenly gleaned the beginnings of a plan.

After checking once more to make sure that his pursuer hadn't entered the alleyway, he hurried over to the grate. He knelt and peered inside. It was too dark to make out much but he thought he saw a small ledge overlooking the rushing water. The rain that had fallen the day before had evidently been heavier than he'd realized.

Benny set his gun down on the ground and pulled out the object that was resting so heavily in his pocket. He looked at it for a few brief seconds and that was enough to give him the shivers. It was a human skull with a horrific looking hole in the roof of it. A bronze nail was embedded in this hole and Benny felt an almost overpowering urge to touch the object. It was an absurd thought, of course, and Benny thought it was probably one that showed just how close to losing it he really was. His life was on the line and here he was, coveting a nail that had been hammered into someone's skull.

Benny pried the grating away from the hole and set it aside. He then leaned over and tried to calculate the trajectory he'd need to ensure that the skull landed on the ledge and didn't fall into the rushing water. He was in the process of letting go when the sound of footsteps directly behind startled him. He slipped ever so slightly, just enough to cause the skull to bounce off the ledge and splash into the water. It bobbed up and down there for a second before vanishing, carried along by the stream.

"What's so important that your friends were willing to die for it, Benny?"

The feminine voice was anything but seductive. It was quite the opposite, in fact. The words were spoken with no trace of empathy at all. Benny might as well as have been a rock, for all this woman cared. Even though she'd said nothing threatening, Benny could tell that she placed absolutely no value on his life.

Benny replaced the covering as quietly as he could and stood up. He'd lost the skull but at least he'd keep it out of her hands. That was a small victory, at least. Turning, he came face-to-face with a sight that was usually the final one for criminals in Atlanta. He saw Dusk, the city's one-woman judge, jury and executioner.

She stood five foot six in flat-heeled shoes. She wore form fitting black trousers, a black bustier covered by a small waist-length coat and a bandito-style mask that covered the lower half of her face. A low-brimmed hat covered the top of her head, allowing a few red-blonde curls of hair to curl around her shoulders. Her eyes were a glittering green and there was something about her entire form that seemed to radiate dangerous sex, a scorching kind of sensuality that left a man feeling both lust and terror in equal amounts. She held a pistol in each hand and Benny, something of a gun nut, recognized the make of them: Smith & Wesson Hand Ejector II. The revolver was introduced a few years before World War I but could still be found in ready supply. Chambered for .45 caliber rounds, the Hand Ejector II normally had a five or six inch barrel but Dusk's guns had modified barrels that had been cut down to four inches in length.

Benny held up both hands, trying to sound braver than he felt. "We were just doin' a job, Dusk. We were paid for a grab and go… and then we was gonna take the loot to the guy who hired us. Nobody was gonna get hurt."

"Tell that to Maxwell Smith. You boys left him with four bullets in his belly while you made off with something from his safe."

Benny instinctively reached for his gun but his hand froze in midair. He glanced down and saw that he'd forgotten to pick it up off the ground after putting the grate back. His eye flicked back to Dusk, who was now advancing towards him.

"Last chance, Benny," she said. "Tell me who hired you and what it was you stole. Or I can just kill you where you stand and find out on my own. Your choice."

Benny didn't take long to make his decision. He charged Dusk, lowering his shoulder in hopes that his greater weight would allow him to knock her aside and gain his freedom. Unfortunately for him, Dusk spun out of the way, extending one of her legs and tripping him up. He hit the ground hard, the impact causing him to bite the tip of his tongue. He struggled to rise, realizing how close he was to death, but Dusk's feet came down on the center of his back. She was remarkably strong and he writhed like a bug that had been pinned to a board.

"How many lives have you ruined?" Dusk asked. Benny whined, especially when he heard the rustle of cloth behind him. He didn't crane his head to see what she was doing. He had a good idea and he didn't want to have his suspicions confirmed.

Benny's friends had gotten off easy. Their lives had been ended by shots from Dusk's pistols, their brains reduced to mush when bullets had ripped through their heads. But Benny knew the vigilante had picked him for a far worse fate.

Dusk took her weight off of him but Benny didn't try to run. Hot tears were suddenly stinging his eyes and he felt moist warmth spread through the crotch of his pants.

"Look at me," Dusk commanded and Benny felt helpless to resist.

Slowly his head came up, his eyes traveling the length of Dusk's svelte body. The mask that had covered the bottom of her face was now loosened, hanging across her chest. Benny's eyes widened as he saw what had been hidden there… his entire body shook as images began to flash before his mind's eye: he saw his first crime, stealing money from his grandmother's purse as a little boy no more than six years old; he witnessed the first time he'd ever raped a woman; his first experience with Opium. So many crimes, great and small… Benny had never realized just what an empty life he'd led.

It was enough to break his fragile hold on reality and, after one prolonged scream that would have chilled the blood of any who heard it, Benny fell into a deep silence. He still breathed and his eyes still blinked, but for all intents and purposes, he could no longer be counted amongst the living. He was lost in an unending contemplation of his sins.

Dusk put her mask back into place and walked over to Benny's fallen gun. She picked it up and examined it briefly before tossing it next to its owner's body. She then moved over to look down into the storm sewer. When she'd entered the alleyway, it had looked like Benny was dropping something down below. She saw nothing, however, meaning that whatever it was had been swept away by the rushing waters.

Beneath her mask, her lips turned downward into a frown. She couldn't return to Smith's home at present – the police would be there and they still considered her just as much a criminal as those she hunted. That meant she wouldn't receive any answers tonight about what the three had stolen or who had hired them.

But tomorrow…

Tomorrow, she would take a new tack in the investigation.

Dusk walked past Benny, feeling no pity for him. He had chosen his path long ago and what she'd done to him did little to balance the scales of justice. Benny's suffering would not undo all the terrible acts he'd committed over the course of his lifetime. Dusk couldn't help but wish she were capable of condemning him to an even worse hell than he was now trapped in.

❊ ❊ ❊

"Look at me," Dusk commanded and Benny felt helpless to resist.

Police Detective Roland Moore stepped through Maxwell Smith's home, unable to keep from staring at the furnishings. There were at least two paintings he'd recognized that would have cost more than two years' salary for him. It was enough to make him think he'd gone into the wrong career.

Following along at Moore's heels was his trusted aide, a slender girl with red-blonde hair named Sue Timlin. She had started out as a simple secretary but she'd soon proven her usefulness beyond typing and filing. She had a keen mind and could look at things from angles that most policemen never would have considered. As such, Moore had begun inviting her along to crime scenes, much to the chagrin of his fellow officers. To say they thought it inappropriate to bring a woman to the scene of a murder was putting it mildly. But Sue had never once lost her cool, not even when presented with the goriest of scenes.

Roland came to a stop next to a chalk outline that had been drawn on the wood floor. It was there that Max Smith had bled out. Someone had placed a call to the authorities, a woman according to the operator, but there had been no one present when the ambulance arrived. Smith was dead by the time they'd reached the house.

Roland caught the eye of a uniformed officer, who hurried over to his side. It was Jenkins, a pasty-skinned youth who was fresh from the academy. Being around kids like Jenkins made Roland feel older than the thirty-five years he'd lived. Roland pointed towards an open safe in the wall. "What was in there?"

"That's the funny thing, detective." Jenkins spoke with a high-pitched squeaky voice that drove Roland nuts. The police detective lit a cigarette while the young man talked. He noticed that Sue was clutching her handbag in front of her long legs and quietly looking about for clues. The fact she was a looker was not lost on Roland but he'd never made any moves on her. He was too afraid it'd ruin their partnership and he'd grown to really appreciate having her around. "They left nearly two thousand dollars in cash. Didn't touch it. The only thing they took was a human skull."

"Smith had a skull in his safe?"

"Yes, sir."

"And how do you know that? Did he leave an inventory of his safe?"

"It was in his will. We found that in the safe. It says that if anything ever happens to him, that the contents of his safe should be given to charity – except for the skull, which is to be burned. We looked… and there's no skull in there now."

Roland glanced at Sue. "Isn't that the damndest thing?"

Sue offered him a pretty smile. She looked as slim and petite as a ballerina but Roland had seen her take down men three times her size with that funny jujitsu stuff she knew. Her green eyes sparkled. "It's not all that strange, really. Max Smith was a member of the Explorer's Club." She gestured at a number of artifacts around the room: a set of spears and a shield from Africa; several pieces of pottery from Peru and a set of ivory elephant tusks. "He probably picked up the skull on one of his adventures."

"Strange that he'd want it destroyed upon his death, though."

Sue shrugged her shoulders. "No stranger than the fact that those thieves would break in here and kill him for it."

"True." Roland moved over to the safe and noted that there were two more chalk outlines here. "So we have any leads on who killed them? Or who placed the call?"

Jenkins grinned so broadly that Roland felt like punching him. "Some of the boys think it was Dusk. Maybe she came up on 'em in the act and plugged 'em, then called for the ambulance."

"And you think she took the skull?"

Jenkins blinked. "I don't know about that."

Roland sighed. He'd already come to the conclusion that Dusk was involved – especially since a crook had been found not far from here, in the sort of catatonic state that was becoming all too familiar. Many cops on the force were beginning to forget that Dusk was as much a criminal as the men she was fighting. There was a reason for rules and laws – they were part of what separated mankind from the animals. Without respect for the rule of law, there was only one thing awaiting everyone: anarchy. "Clear everybody out of here," Roland said.

Jenkins nodded, hurriedly moving all of the other investigators and the guys from the coroner's office into another room. He didn't bother trying to remove Sue – everybody on the force knew that Roland would want her to stick with him.

Roland puffed away on his cigarette while staring at the open safe. "What do you think, Sue?"

Sue clasped her hands behind her back, purse still held tightly in her fingers. She approached Roland with pursed lips, a habit he recognized. She always pursed her lips when she was working something out in that pretty head of hers. "We need to go through his papers. You remember last year when the Atlanta Journal ran that bio piece on Smith? They said he was working on a book detailing all of his exploits. It stands to reason that he might have mentioned that skull in his journals."

"Let's get to it, then. Hopefully those goons from the station haven't trampled all over any evidence we might need."

Sue moved away, picking up papers and flipping through them. Smith had evidently been an avid reader for there were magazines and books on a wide of variety of subjects lying about. She was a voracious reader herself and so she recognized many of the authors and titles.

"Found it," Roland said. He was wearing a triumphant grin and Sue found herself laughing at him. His face fell and she immediately realized she'd hurt his feelings. "What?" he asked.

"You just looked so happy."

"Well, I should be. I think this is exactly what we wanted." He held up a small black leather-bound book. "It's a diary."

"I think when men keep one of those, it's called a journal." Sue took it from his hands and flipped through it. It was mostly written in a modified version of shorthand and consisted of dates, names and brief notes of what occurred. She noticed the final entry was dated last night at 8 o'clock, meaning it was only a few hours before Smith's murder:

Have decided against including the missionary's story in the book. Too dangerous. Marquard knows I have it and the story would only confirm it. Best to destroy things and forget it ever happened.

Roland plucked the book from her fingertips. He dropped it into the pocket of his coat. "I'll read over this back at the office." He cleared his throat. "You free for dinner tonight? We can talk over the case."

Sue smiled. "Can't. I have to leave as soon as work is over. Visiting an old friend in Savannah."

"Oh. You taking tomorrow off?"

"Of course not. I can't leave you to handle things on your own. You'd be likely to fall apart without me."

"I can't argue with you there," Roland admitted. "It's just a lot of driving for one night. You want me to tag along? Two sets of hands on the wheel are better than one."

"You're sweet, Roland. But not this time." Sue turned away from her friend and partner, her mind turning over the words from the journal. *Who was Marquard? Was he the key to the entire affair?* She knew she wouldn't get any rest until she knew the answer to that.

Chapter II.
Glumm

Savannah, Georgia

Dusk slammed her elbow into the crook's face, shattering the man's nose. She then grabbed hold of her opponent's arm and swung him about, sending him tumbling into the arms of the other three thugs. All four men hit the ground and Dusk rushed forward, kicking two in their faces before they could defend themselves. She then raised the butt of her pistol and brought it crashing down onto the skull of another. That left only the one with the broken nose. Dusk regarded him for a moment before walking past him, leaving the man to whine in pain.

The door leading to the home of Phineas Glumm swung open and a cadaverous-looking man stood there, with hands on hips. "Dusk," the man said with a most unfriendly smile. "You could have just knocked, you know."

Phineas Glumm was Savannah's most disturbing resident. A transplanted Briton, Glumm had made his fortune in the ivory field before retiring to Georgia. At one time, he'd had nearly a hundred poachers in his employ, all of them given a single task: hunt down and kill as many elephants as possible, depriving the dead and dying animals of their tusks in the process. It was nasty work but Glumm himself had never been witness to it: he'd remained in England the whole time, enjoying his three vices: wine, women and witchcraft.

"Your guards didn't seem to want to let me pass," Dusk said, stepping past Glumm. The interior of the house smelled strongly of incense. A massive oil panting of a reclining nude woman dominated the foyer and Dusk wondered at what sort of man would make sure that such artwork was the first thing his guests saw upon entering.

"They probably remembered you from your last visit," Glumm said, shutting the door behind him. He didn't seem overly concerned about his injured men. "I'm sure you remember… you burst in unannounced and demanded information from me. Much like now, I'd imagine."

Dusk kept walking until she'd reached Glumm's study. The room was wood-paneled, with a tiger skin rug on the floor. The smell of incense was strongest here and Dusk visibly winced a bit at the strength of the odor. Her eyes drifted across the spines of numerous old books, some of which bore titles in Latin. "There's a mystery in Atlanta and I want your help in understanding it."

Glumm smiled softly and sat down in a large-backed chair. He gestured for Dusk to take a seat on a nearby couch but the vigilante answered with a shake of her head. "Why me?" Glumm asked. "Surely you have limitless resources in your so-called war on crime."

"I really missed visiting Savannah."

Glumm laughed softly. "Very well, my mysterious friend. Tell me of this mystery and I shall do my best to illuminate you about its meaning."

Dusk recounted all that she knew, speaking slowly. Glumm said nothing in response, merely closing his eyes. He almost looked like he'd fallen asleep but Dusk knew better. The man had a mind like a steel trap and he was no doubt sifting through all the details, looking for some clue to fasten on.

When she was finished, Glumm remained motionless for a full minute before opening his eyes. "I can help you, I believe." Glumm smiled. "But I want something in return."

"I'm not here to make deals."

"But you do need assistance. And I can give it. All I want is a small trifle, nothing that would put you out."

"Go on."

"I know this Marquard," Glumm said. "He is a foul man, well-muscled and swarthy. He is an oily fellow – his hair always looks like he needs to wash it. You know the sort?" Glumm shrugged when Dusk did not reply. "About six years ago, he contacted me, wanting information on The Fourth Nail. I gave it to him and not long after, he helped finance an expedition to Budapest in search of it."

Dusk moved closer now, her eyes fixed on the gaunt man in front of her. "I've never heard of anything called The Fourth Nail."

"I'm not surprised. It's a rather obscure piece of Christian myth. You see, there were originally four nails that were set aside for use in the crucifixion of Christ: two for his hands, one for his feet and one for his heart. That last nail would, of course, have ended his suffering quickly."

"Marquard was looking for the nail that was supposed to be used on Christ's heart?"

"Yes. You see, according to the story, a gypsy stole The Fourth Nail and used it to repair his wagon. The gypsy didn't know what he'd done but God was pleased. He wanted the world to see his son suffer, so that his resurrection would be all the more enduring. God blessed The Fourth Nail, ensuring that anyone who held it would have his or her worldly sins forgiven. Furthermore, the owner of The Nail would be immune to illness or age. They could still be killed, mind you, but they would not die of natural causes."

"Smith went with Marquard on this expedition," Dusk said. It was more of a statement than a question, so Glumm merely grunted his assent and continued on.

"My guess – and here I am delving into the always dangerous world of conjecture – is that Smith found The Fourth Nail and kept it a secret from Marquard. He brought it back to Atlanta and hid it in his safe."

"That doesn't add up," Dusk countered. "Those thieves didn't steal a nail – they took a human skull."

"Nevertheless, it fits. From all accounts, Smith was an extraordinarily fit man for his age. Perhaps he would have lived forever if the nail hadn't been stolen from him?"

Dusk said nothing but Glumm could tell that her mind was working over what he had told her. "What do you want in return?" she finally asked.

Glumm cleared his throat and his hands came together, the fingers moving nervously. "I want to see your face."

"No."

"It's just that I've heard the stories… and I'm curious to see if they're true."

"To look at my uncovered face is to see your true nature revealed. All your past sins will be revisited. There are few men in the world who can look at me and emerge unscathed."

"I confess that I welcome the challenge."

Dusk nodded slowly. "If it's what you want, I'll grant the request. But I don't understand why you would do this." The vigilante reached up to loosen the veil that hid the lower part of her face, letting it fall away. Glumm's eyes widened at what he saw but his reaction was far from the norm. Rather than screaming or crying, he merely smiled, as if he were seeing something he already knew. Dusk stared at the man for a moment before hiding her face once more.

"Astonishing," Glumm murmured. He leaned back in his chair, somewhat unsteadily. He saw the confusion in Dusk's eyes and laughed. "I am very self-aware man, my friend. All my sins are well known to me. I have long ago come to terms with who and what I am."

"That makes you all the more despicable then. You have no heart to feel remorse with."

Glumm shrugged his slender shoulders. "Perhaps I simply don't need you to damn me. I can do that all by myself." He rose and offered a mocking bow. "And now our transactions are at an end, I assume?"

Dusk moved towards the door, speaking as she walked. "Just remember that I'm watching you. Keep your nose clean or I'll cut it off."

"I shall do that. Oh – one more thing, if you don't mind?"

"Make it quick, Glumm." Dusk paused in the doorway, turning her body to face the information broker.

"You should watch yourself. You're making a lot of very powerful men in Atlanta quite nervous. They're likely to try and snuff you out. I've heard they're even talking about bringing in outside help."

"Why the warning?"

Glumm looked the very picture of innocence. "If something were to happen to you, I'd miss these little chats of ours."

❀ ❀ ❀

Thaddeus Marquard ran a hand through his greasy hair and clenched his jaw. He was a big man, one whose tailored suit looked out of place on him. He had a bestial air about him and people who saw him were often reminded of a jungle cat. As such, being in a civilized manner of dress looked out of place. It was far easier to picture Marquard in a loincloth.

"I don't get this," he said at last, pacing back and forth behind the ma-hogany desk that dominated his office. The man who stood uncomfortably before him shifted his weight from foot to foot, bracing himself for Marquard's fury. Larry Sands had worked for Marquard for over three years and he'd grown accustomed to the man's mercurial moods. "How the hell did this Dusk dame get wind of what we were doing?"

"No idea, boss. But if the skull's out there, we're gonna find it. Our sources at inside the police department say that Benny didn't have it on him when they found his body, so either he stashed it someplace or Dusk took it."

Marquard stopped his pacing, staring out the window with his back to Larry. Outside, he could see the citizens of Atlanta scurrying back and forth as their day got underway. Having an office on Peachtree Street meant that he got to see a cross-section of the city at all times: the wealthy and the poor all congregated together in the heart of the city. "Do you have any idea of how many people I've killed, Larry?"

"Not a clue, boss."

"A lot. More than I can count." Marquard watched a young mother pushing a stroller down the sidewalk. "My momma used to say I was born evil and I think she may have been right. I mean, we've all got that Original Sin but I was worse than most. I strangled my puppy when I was three years old. I told my daddy that our hired hand did it. My daddy whipped that Negro within an inch of his life and I just smiled the whole time."

Larry cleared his throat but said nothing. He wasn't sure where his boss was going with this but the tone of it wasn't like anything he'd heard from Marquard before. The big man was usually one for ranting and raving, along with a good dose

"How the hell did you do that?" he asked.

of punching. But this sounded oddly philosophical and it unsettled Larry greatly.

"I killed my own mother," Marquard added in a flat tone of voice. "That alone should cause me to burn in hell, don't you think?"

"I ain't much for church, boss," Larry said when the silence lingered long enough for him to realize that it wasn't a rhetorical question. "But I think murderin' anybody is a sin, especially your mom."

Marquard laughed, shaking his head. "You're a genius, you know that?" He turned back to Larry then and the look in his eyes showed that things were back on more familiar ground now. Marquard looked dangerous again, like he might throw himself across the desk and throttle his subordinate. As a result, Larry took one step backward. "I want that skull and I want it as soon as possible, Larry. If I don't have it on my desk by tomorrow morning, I'm going to have you castrated. Do you know what that means?"

"Yeah, boss. I know what means."

"Good. Then get the hell out of here and get me that skull!" Marquard watched as Larry hurried from the room, shouting at the man's retreating back, "And send Doc Severin in here!"

Severin passed Larry on the other man's way out. A short man with a baldhead and oversized glasses, the doctor would have looked comical if not for the grave expression he perpetually wore. "You bellowed, Mr. Marquard?"

Marquard ignored the doctor's tone. He took a deep breath and waited for the man to close the door behind him. "My head's killing me, doc. I need something."

"You're already taking the most powerful medicines I can give you. Anything stronger and you'd be incapable of running your business affairs."

Marquard closed his eyes and ground his teeth together. He was dying and there was nothing anyone could do. That was why he needed that skull and, more importantly, the nail that had been driven into it. Without it, he was on a one-way track to Hell.

Doc Severin moved closer to the desk, reaching into his coat pocket and pulling forth a small bottle of pills. "Here. Take this for now. It will numb you for a bit but shouldn't impair your faculties."

Marquard snatched the pills away and smiled. "Thanks, doc. I owe you one."

Severin's eyes sparkled in response.

Chapter III.
Roland and the Skull

Detective Roland Moore ignored the stares that accompanied his entrance onto the playground. There were few real kids around as the area had become home to a bunch of teenaged hoodlums, who played dice and cards while sipping from brown bags filled with stuff they were too young to purchase legally. Roland had been here many times in recent months, mostly to put the fear of the law in the kids, hoping it would scare some of them straight. So far, it hadn't proven very successful – but the call he'd gotten upon arriving at the station this morning gave him new hope. It had been so noteworthy that he'd set aside the plans he'd made to visit Marquard at his office.

He stopped in the center of the playground and lit a cigarette. After shaking out the match and tossing it aside, he asked, "So which of you kids is Reggie?"

A slender boy of about fourteen stepped out of the crowd, his acne-ridden face bearing an odd expression. Roland realized that he'd seen something like it before: when he was growing up and attending church regularly, he'd often seen this look on the face of the elders when they'd 'feel the presence of the Lord.' Roland had assumed they were all faking it since he'd never felt anything but boredom. But Reggie certainly looked like he was glowing from within as he walked towards the detective, a wooden box clutched tightly in his left hand.

"That would be me, sir."

There was something so respectful in the boy's tone that Roland was momentarily taken aback. He was sure he recognized Reggie as one of the most belligerent of the hoodlums. "You called the station and said you'd found something important. Something related to the murder that was mentioned in the papers this morning. That true?"

"Yes. I found what you're looking for. I found the missing skull."

Roland stared hard at the young man. The paper had talked about the murder and had mentioned that several items had been taken. It had even contained references to Dusk's involvement in things. But it had not even hinted that one of the missing items was a human skull. "How'd you know we were looking for a skull, kid?"

"It told me. The Nail." Reggie held out the box to Roland and the friendly smile the boy wore grew broader. "When you touch it, you'll understand."

Roland swallowed and he realized that his heart was pounding. He didn't understand it – he'd faced hardened killers and wandered through crime scenes that would have turned the stomachs of lesser men but here he was feeling true fear over the prospect of taking this box from a young boy. He reached out and took it, tossing aside his cigarette so he could hold it with both hands. There was warmth coming from within that made his fingertips tingle. Without looking at Reggie, he flipped open the lid of the box and saw a human skull with a large nail embedded in it. The nail had been driven in with such force that it had caused the skull to crack in several places. If the skull's owner wasn't dead when the blow was administered, he would have been afterwards.

"I found it when it washed out of one of the sewer lines," Reggie said. "At first I thought it would look great in one of our clubhouses, you know, to scare people and stuff. But as soon as I touched it, I knew I wasn't ever going to be the same again. It was like being born all over again!"

Roland wondered how a kid Reggie's age would know anything about stuff like that. He decided not to ask and instead reached into the box and gripped the skull, lifting it free. The strange tingling he felt before was stronger now and he could feel it in his teeth, humming away. But it was when his fingers brushed The Fourth Nail itself that the full effect hit him.

Immediately, he felt a strange energy flow through him. He felt like his minor injuries were fading away like a memory and, even more importantly, that his spirit was being lightened. Little things that he felt guilty over suddenly seemed forgotten and all the petty sins he'd committed over his lifetime didn't seem quite so important any longer. As Reggie had said, it was like being born anew. Roland pictured himself covered in filth, stepping into the pouring rain. The rain washed away all the grime, leaving his skin pink and new. It was liberating and awe-inspiring. For someone who had always doubted the presence of any force greater than himself, it was a revelation. This was genuinely the power of a higher being.

Roland was shaking when he looked back at Reggie. "That was incredible."

The young boy nodded eagerly. "I'm going back home today. I ran away months ago but now… I think I can work things out with my pa. I really do."

Roland was about to say something when two dark-garbed men entered the playground area. The kids obviously recognized them because the air was suddenly filled with tension. The two men were familiar to Roland, too. He recognized them from various mug shots he'd seen over the years. The bigger of the two had a block-shaped head and was named Mort, the smaller was a weasel-looking sort named Carl.

The two men headed straight towards Roland, their eyes fixed on the skull in his hand. Mort's hand dipped into his jacket and did not re-emerge. Meanwhile, Carl applied one of the most fake smiles that Roland had ever borne witness to.

"Detective!" Carl said, clapping his hands together as if he were actually glad to see the man. "What a surprise. We were just coming down here to speak to our nephews. They told us that they'd found something that belonged to us… and there it is now! Thanks for keeping it warm for us, Detective."

Reggie shot a withering look at a few of the other boys, who looked away shamefaced. All of the youths sometimes did jobs for the local crime bosses and evidently one or more of them had contacted a few gangs to see if they'd want to pay something for the skull.

Roland didn't show any fear in front of the toughs, despite being quite aware that he was outnumbered. He slipped the skull back into its box and then raised his chin. "This skull doesn't belong to either of you and we all know it. It's part of an ongoing criminal investigation so if you still want to lay claim to it, you're welcome to come down to the station and answer a few questions."

Carl laughed and nudged Mort. "The Detective's a real comedian, eh?"

"He's hilarious," Mort rumbled.

"The Nail's not meant for people like you," Reggie blurted out. Before Roland could react, Carl had backhanded the boy hard enough to send him tumbling to the ground.

"Shut your mouth, you little gutter rat!"

Roland saw Reggie's lower lip dripping crimson and he started to reach for his gun when Mort drew his own piece, smirking as Roland's hand froze in place.

"Can I plug him, Carl?" Mort asked, his desires evident in the gleam of his eyes.

"I wouldn't try that," a soft female voice said, just as the barrel of a gun was pressed against the back of Mort's head. "Not unless you want to die along with him."

Carl blinked in surprise, motioning for Mort to lower his weapon. Sue had joined the group, moving so quietly that not even Roland had heard her approach. The dainty-looking young woman held a slim handgun in her right hand and her face showed no hesitation about using it. "Who the hell are you, girlie?"

"I work for Detective Moore," she answered sweetly. "Should we take them in, boss?"

Roland grinned, pulling out his gun and waved it at Carl, who reluctantly raised his hands over his head. "Sounds like a plan, doll. A real fine one, at that."

It was the brutish Mort who reacted with a roar. He slammed his body backwards, causing Sue's hand to fly up. She squeezed the trigger as she did so and the bullet whizzed by the thug's head, narrowly missing it. Carl lunged for Roland, delivering a powerful punch that sent the detective to the ground. Carl snatched up the box containing the skull and took off at a quick sprint, leaving Mort to deal with his would-be pursuers.

The big man delivered a kick to Roland's stomach that knocked all the air from his lungs. The detective rolled onto his hands and knees, struggling to get back to his feet. His head was ringing and he felt a sharp pain with every intake of breath, making him wonder if Mort had cracked a rib with that kick. He heard Sue saying something but with the ringing of his ears, he wasn't sure what it was. He slowly pushed off the ground, staggering upright. For a moment, his vision dimmed and he feared he was about to pass out but he regained control of his body and whirled about, prepared to offer Sue some assistance.

His mouth gaped open when he saw Sue standing with one foot on Mort's chest. The big man was on his back, unconscious. He had a bright red bruise on the center of his neck and Roland saw that it was vaguely foot-shaped. "How the hell did you do that?" he asked.

Sue stepped back and smoothed down her skirt. "He didn't take me seriously so I caught him by surprise with a kick."

"Boy, I'll say!" exclaimed Reggie, moving closer. His lip still looked bad but he was staring at Sue like she was an angel. "I never saw anybody outside The Rockettes kick that high!"

"I used to take dance," Sue said, looking in the direction that Carl had fled. "He's probably long gone by now." Putting her hands on her slim hips, she turned back to Roland. "Why don't you call the station and put out an APB on him and then we'll stop by my apartment. It's only a few blocks from here and I can give you something for the pain."

Roland nodded, wincing as he took a step towards her. He felt like an idiot, having lost the skull. Something that precious shouldn't be in the hands of men like that. He looked down at Mort and grimaced. "He's going to be a handful fitting into the car."

"We can watch him," Reggie offered. "Until the paddy wagon comes for him, I mean."

Roland considered the offer and finally nodded. He trusted the boy implicitly now. They'd both touched the Fourth Nail… and that bonded them somehow. "Be careful. If he starts to wake up, just give him a good sock to the noggin."

The look on Reggie's face suggested that he'd have no qualms about doing just that.

❀ ❀ ❀

Roland had never been in Sue's apartment before and he couldn't help but look around himself with open curiosity. If she noticed, she didn't seem to mind and she left him alone in the living room while she went to fetch him some aspirin. The décor was distinctively feminine, with soft pastels and a predominance of pink but there were a few signs that Sue was no stereotypical girl: a few police procedure handbooks and a rather racy-looking true crime magazine lay in open view. But it was the walls that kept Roland's attention as he waited for his associate to return. He saw pictures of her through various stages of her life and he was intrigued that she seemed to be of two spirits: in some of the photos she wore the open, engaging smile with which he was so familiar. In others, though, she seemed much more dour, with dark rings about her eyes and a sullen expression. Two pictures in particular seemed to say much about this dichotomy: in each she appeared to be about 14 years old but in one she was smiling at the beach, her long hair blowing in the breeze. In the other, her hair was much shorter, cut in a bob. In this photo, she stared out at Roland with the expression of one whose best friend had just died. Strangely, the background of the photo suggested that she was standing on the pier of a beach. Was it the same one where the happier photo had been taken? If so, it couldn't have been taken very long after the first. What had transpired to change her mood so much?

"Here you go."

Roland turned, feeling like he'd been caught spying in her medicine cabinet. He took the two white pills she held in her hand and popped them into his mouth and then he washed them down with a glass of water she also provided.

"Dusk was in Savannah last night," Sue said, taking a seat on the couch. Roland joined her, leaving a cushion between them.

"You're kidding me," he said. "Did you see her?"

"Yes. She stopped me when I was on the way out of town."

Roland forgot all about the pain he'd been feeling. He'd never come face-to-face with the mysterious Dusk but he'd heard from others who had. They told of an alluring but highly dangerous figure, one that inspired more fear than desire. "What did she want?"

"She said she was investigating the Marquard case, just like we were. Said she was willing to share some of her findings with me."

"Did she want to make some kind of deal?"

"Not that she said. I think she just wanted to make sure that justice was done."

"Was she as scary as everyone says?"

Sue laughed and Roland blinked in surprise. When she saw the hurt look on his face, she quickly composed herself. "No. Not really. She's not a ghost or anything like that. She's just a woman, not much different than me. Well, except for the guns and mask. I wasn't scared, no."

"I've heard she's a stone cold killer."

"I'm sure she is but I didn't sense that she meant me any harm. She wants to make sure Marquard is caught."

"So what did she tell you?" There was something in Roland's tone that made it clear that he wasn't going to be altogether trusting of Dusk's words but Sue had expected that.

She recounted the origins of The Fourth Nail, as well as the suspicions that Dusk had about how Maxwell Smith had come to own it. When she was finished, Roland sat back on the couch and pursed his lips thoughtfully. "You think she's on the level with this, don't you?"

"Don't you?"

"If you'd asked me that an hour ago, I'd have said no. I don't believe in spiritualism. But after touching that skull with the nail in it, I don't know what I think. It changed me. Made me feel like a new man. It was incredible."

Sue looked thoughtful for a moment. "I wonder why a man like Marquard would want it."

"Maybe he wants to be immortal. That's not a strange desire."

"In a line of work like his, I'd think it's more likely he's going to die violently – and The Fourth Nail wouldn't stop that."

Roland grunted at that. "We need to get to Marquard's place."

"Do we have a warrant to search his office?"

"Not yet but it's coming. In the meantime, we can make sure he knows we are on to him. Maybe it'll scare him into making a mistake. All we need is to find a direct link to the murder, something to show he sent those guys to do the job."

Sue looked away for a moment, obviously thinking something through. While her head was turned, Roland took the opportunity to admire the graceful curve of her neck and the smoothness of her skin. He averted his gaze a second too slow and she caught his appreciative glance when she looked back at him. "I'm glad you're not too badly hurt. I wish you wouldn't go into situations without backup. It's dangerous and you've made a lot of enemies."

Roland bristled a bit, though he knew she meant well. "I'm a man who can take care of himself, doll." He stood up. "But if it makes you feel better, come along and back me up when I face Marquard."

Chapter IV.
An Accumulation of Sins

Thaddeus Marquard licked his lips in anticipation. The box containing The Fourth Nail sat before him on his desk. It was unopened but he had felt the weight of it when he'd taken it from Carl, making sure that the man knew he was going to be richly rewarded for his efforts. The tingling sensation that had passed through him while holding the box had confirmed all the stories for Marquard: he was on the verge of salvation.

That was the key to all his current activities. Over the years, he'd accumulated so many sins that he was directly bound for Hell. The existence of The Fourth Nail could be seen as proof that the biblical stories were at least partially true and that meant that there probably was a place of eternal damnation. Marquard wanted to avoid that fate. Even if his physical condition continued to deteriorate – and according to legend, that might not be the case, for The Fourth Nail was supposed to provide a certain degree of healing properties upon its owner – he would die with a clean slate on his soul. If there was a Hell, there was bound to be a Heaven, after all. Marquard would be welcomed into the Pearly Gates on a technicality, perhaps, but he wasn't beyond working the system.

Leaning forward with shaking hands, Marquard slowly opened the box. The first thing he saw was the top of The Fourth Nail, protruding up from the roof of the skull. The previous owner of The Nail had put up a fierce struggle over the sacred relic and in a fit of anger Maxwell Smith had plucked up a hammer and driven The Nail down into the man's skull. Almost immediately, Max had changed, filled with guilt and something that Marquard couldn't quite name. Until that moment, neither Max nor Marquard had touched the Nail and both considered it an object worth selling, rather than keeping for its supposed magical properties. Marquard had focused on claiming various other objects as prizes while Max supervised the handling of The Fourth Nail. But on the way back to the States, the Nail had, according to Max, disappeared. At first, Marquard believed that Max intended to sell it and keep the profits for himself but over time, his opinion changed. He began to believe that Max believed in The Nail's properties. Why he'd never removed it from the skull was beyond Marquard's ability to fathom.

He was about to reach in and touch the sacred object when the door to his office opened and Doc Severin entered. "Have you ever heard of knocking, Doc?"

"Sorry to interrupt. I was told that you'd decided to not take your afternoon medicines. I think that's a bad idea."

Marquard stood up, his eyes narrowing. "I appreciate how attentive to my needs you've been, doctor, but I think it might be time for us to have a little chat."

Severin stopped short of the desk, his normally placid face taking on a new cast. It was one of worry. "What do you mean?"

"I was willing to turn a blind eye while you treated my illness, despite the fact that you often crossed the boundaries I set with my other employees. It was in your best interest to keep me alive, so I trusted you to do that. But I don't need you anymore."

"Your condition," Severin began but Marquard cut him off with a raised hand.

"Is no longer your concern. You've told me numerous times that my condition isn't going to get better. All I can do is make my last days relatively pain free. True?"

"Yes, but I think that you should continue your treatments."

"Of course you do. The longer I live, the more you get paid." Marquard gestured towards The Fourth Nail. "The item in that box is going to help me become pure again, Doctor Severin. It might even cure me. So I don't need your services any longer."

Severin tensed, obviously expecting Marquard to take up arms against him. Very few people left the man's employ with their lives intact. To his tremendous surprise, however, Marquard came around the desk and put an arm around his shoulders, steering him towards his closet door.

"I'd like to keep you on retainer," Marquard was saying. "But to be honest, if I die, as long as I've avoid Hell, I'll be fine. I do plan to go out with a bang, though. Want to see what I mean?"

Severin nodded, still uncertain about his fate. Was he really being let go without any physical harm coming to him?

Marquard threw open the closet door and reached inside, pushing aside mounds of paper and several spare jackets. He came back with an oversized leather glove that featured a metal ring around the wrist. Dotting the edges of the ring were small raised buttons that were connected to one another by thin electrical wire. "I bought this from a man named Luger. He lives in Sovereign City and has a team of scientists on his payroll. They're in the business of making super weapons. This is a very expensive item called a Thunderfist." Marquard pulled the glove onto his right hand and clenched his fingers together. As soon as he did so, the wires began to hum and tiny sparks of electricity jumped about, eventually forming a circuit around the base of the glove.

"What in heaven's name?" Severin whispered, taking a step away from Marquard.

"It generates a field that will fry just about anything it touches. And I can knock my way through a brick wall with it, too."

"But what do you plan to do with it?"

"I'm going to start by consolidating the gangs under my control. Kill a few guys and the rest will fall into line. Once I'm in control of this town, I start putting pressure on the folks in charge: the police chief, the mayor, and the newspaper publishers. I'm going to become King of Atlanta."

Severin said nothing, realizing that Marquard was even more insane than he'd ever believed. The man believed that something in that box on his desk was going to save his soul, leading him to embark on some scheme to use an electricity-generating glove to take over Atlanta.

Marquard looked towards Severin, as if sensing the man's doubt. "Something bothering you?"

Severin took a deep breath, knowing that he shouldn't criticize Marquard at this juncture but unable to stop himself. "If that thing does cure you... or at the very least, is able to offer you some form of spiritual salvation... then why throw that away on some new criminal plot? Shouldn't you embrace your new life and become a better man?"

"I want to leave something behind, Doc. I don't have any kids that I know about so if I want to have a legacy, it's got to be one that I made, you know what I'm saying? People in this town are going to remember Thaddeus Marquard and his Thunderfist."

"And you're going to do all of that with a glove?"

"Not just a glove. This is just something personal I bought at the same time as my real treasure. It's too big to fit into this office but right now it's strapped onto the bottom of a zeppelin that's going to fly over the city tomorrow, right when the mayor's giving his press conference to announce the hiring of twenty new police officers." Marquard moved quickly away from the still stunned Severin and yanked open a drawer on his desk. He pulled out a photograph, which he brandished proudly. "Take a look-see."

Severin stared at the odd device for several seconds before blinking. It looked like the barrel of a gun, though far larger, measuring nearly twelve feet in length. A series of buttons along the shaft of the object resembled those on Marquard's Thunderfist glove. "Are you trying to tell me that this is a giant version of that glove?"

"You got it. It can fire a burst of electricity capable of frying dozens, if not hundreds, of people all at once. I'm gonna be like Zeus, Doc, sending down my thunderbolts to slay my enemies."

Not knowing what else to say, Doctor Severin muttered, "Brilliant."

He was saved from further discussion by a knock on the door. A pretty young blonde, Marquard's personal secretary, peeked into the room. "Sorry to bother you, sir, but there's an officer here to see you. His name is Roland Moore."

Marquard's smile faded. He dismissed Severin with a quick wave and returned to his desk, placing both the photo and the box containing The Fourth Nail into a drawer. He didn't notice the relief evident on Severin's face and wouldn't have cared if he had.

His ultimate victory was approaching and nothing would ruin it, especially not some two-bit cop.

❄ ❄ ❄

Roland and Sue were ushered into Marquard's office and both of them felt like the proverbial flies wandering too close to the spider's web. There were two men outside the building and despite the fact that they appeared to be absorbed in the daily paper, Roland knew they were guns for hire. They passed three more like them in the lobby and another two who were sitting in the waiting room outside. Heck, Roland felt reasonably certain that the secretary was packing, too.

Sue was a bit more concerned with the man they'd passed on their way in. She knew him: Doctor Severin, a man whose medical license had been yanked three years ago after he'd been busted on ethics charges. It was that sort of perfect recall that made her so valuable to Roland.

Thaddeus Marquard didn't bother getting up from his chair. He seemed to be engrossed in several sheets of bars and graphs. Without looking up, he asked, "So what can I do for you, Detective?"

Roland didn't bother pretending to be nice. He deliberately leaned across the desk, obscuring Marquard's view of the papers. "An old friend of yours was murdered and a few things were stolen from his safe. You know anything about that?"

"If you're talking about Maxwell, I've heard about it. It was in the papers. A shame, though the man and I had a falling out a few years ago and hadn't really kept in touch."

"That why you didn't feel bad about having him killed?"

"If you're making accusations like that, maybe I should call my lawyer."

Roland straightened, a look of venom on his face. "I had a nasty run-in with a guy named Mort not long ago. His buddy managed to slip away with a box containing a human skull. I want it. Give it to me now and maybe I'll give you a head start in getting out of town before I come after you."

Sue looked at Roland in surprise, wondering if he was serious. Did he want to get The Fourth Nail back so badly that he'd bend the law to do it?

Marquard snorted. "Please. I don't believe you, Detective... and even if I did, I don't know anything about a box with a skull in it. Why would I want a skull?"

"You want The Fourth Nail," Roland said, carefully watching the criminal for any signs of recognition. Marquard's face remained devoid of any traces of guilt. "You think that's going to wash away all your sins?" Roland pressed. "Because I think the blood's so deeply ingrained in your skin that nothing would remove the stench."

"Do you have papers giving you the authority to search my office, Detective? Because if you don't, I suggest you turn around and leave, taking your pet girl with you. If you stay any longer, I might press charges against you for harassment."

Roland clenched his fists. "Why you—"

Sue caught Roland by the arm. "Let it go." Casting a disapproving look at Marquard, she added, "We're sorry to have bothered you, Mr. Marquard. If you think of anything that might help us solve Mr. Smith's murder, please contact us at the station."

Without waiting for a response, Sue began tugging Roland towards the door. When they were in the elevator, he pulled away and asked incredulously, "What was that about? I was starting to get to him!"

"You were close to getting yourself thrown in jail. We can come back once we've got the warrant." Sue bit her bottom lip and looked mischievously at her friend. "Or, I could ask Dusk to handle it. Then we don't need a warrant at all."

"You didn't say she'd left you her number."

"She told me how to contact her, as long as I promised not to share that information."

Roland regarded her with an odd expression on his face. "Not even with me?"

"Not even you. She… doesn't really trust men. I think something bad happened to her once and that's part of the reason why she does all this."

Roland stuffed his hands into the pockets of his pants and stepped out into the lobby when the elevator door opened. "Fine. Give her a call. See if she can do something. But you and I never had this conversation."

Sue looked at him brightly. "What conversation?"

Roland found himself grinning. "That's my girl."

Chapter V.
The Lord of Lightning

It was near midnight when Thaddeus Marquard strode into the hangar containing his zeppelin. The airship was moored with long ropes, giving the impression that the zeppelin was some mighty creature of the sky, ensnared in some awful prison that kept it earthbound. The villain held the box in his right hand, The Fourth Nail still buried in the skull of its old owner. He had yet to actually touch the holy relic. Something kept stopping him, though he couldn't quite explain what it was. It was almost as if the anticipation of salvation was so sweet that he couldn't quite bring himself to end the process.

There was also the fact that Roland's words had disturbed him. What if his sins were so great that nothing could wash them away? How would he deal with that disappointment?

Rather than answer any of those questions, he chose to keep the box close at hand and go about his duties. He had brought along The Thunderfist, thinking it fitting that he should have it when boarding the zeppelin. He carried it in a small duffel bag in his left hand.

A slender German with thin blond hair, a long white coat and round glasses, was berating members of the flight crew when Marquard entered. The man paused and forced a smile on his face at the sight of his patron. Professor Wilhelm Hohmann bowed low in greeting. "Herr Marquard! This is a surprise! We did not expect you at this hour!"

"Is everything ready for the morning?"

"But of course! The mayor is scheduled to give his speech at ten a.m. and our zeppelin will be airborne a half hour before that!"

Marquard studied the vessel proudly, like a father viewing a newborn son. "And there won't be any problems?"

"None. It has been tested quite thoroughly!"

"Good. Because if anything does go wrong, I'm going to blame you." Marquard saw the German's smile fade slightly and he laughed, slapping the man on the back. "I'd like to step onboard. I haven't been on it since I purchased it and you began making the modifications."

Hohmann nodded briskly, barking at his men to help Marquard board his ship. His words broke off in mid-sentence, however, and a millisecond later, a crack rang out in the air. Marquard was looking directly at Hohmann when a hole in the man's throat seemed to magically appear, blood spilling quickly out. The German raised his hands in a vain attempt to stop the bleeding but he quickly sagged to his knees, gurgling his next few words.

Marquard dove up the stairs leading onto the zeppelin. He turned around to see a woman entering the hangar, a gun in each hand. Her accuracy was uncanny and within seconds, Marquard saw four more of his men fall to the ground, all with wounds to their heads or chests.

The woman was so stunning that Marquard was momentarily rooted to the spot. She looked average height but her body was tight and hard, encased in tight black trousers and a black bustier that showcased ample cleavage. The lower half of her face was hidden beneath a cloth mask and her low-brimmed hat hid all but a few red-blonde curls. Though he'd never seen her before, Marquard knew instantly that he was looking at the infamous Dusk.

He almost felt flattered to see her here.

Dusk approached the zeppelin without fear, reloading as she went. The few men she hadn't shot had ducked behind barrels or other equipment. None of them were armed, not having expected any trouble. "Thaddeus Marquard," she yelled. "It's time to face justice."

Marquard set down the box and opened the duffel bag, quickly donning The Thunderfist. He stepped down the ramp, moving into Dusk's view. She was holding her guns at her side, both barrels trailing smoke. "If you're here about Maxwell, you've got the wrong person," he said.

"We both know better than that." Dusk's green eyes fastened onto the strange glove that Marquard wore. "Your fashion sense is as bad as your morals."

Marquard grunted. "Funny. No one mentioned that you had a sense of humor."

"That's because they're all dead."

Marquard snarled. He hated anyone who didn't bow down before him but he particularly detested mouthy women. Acting with surprising speed, Marquard charged Dusk, activating The Thunderfist as he moved. It crackled to life, sparks flying as he closed in on his opponent. Dusk moved as gracefully as a cat and avoided him for the most part but Marquard caught her shoulder with the edge of his glove.

The electrical impact was enough to elicit a grunt of pain from the vigilante and it lifted her off her feet, sending her flying backwards. She landed in a crouch, her arm numb down to the elbow.

"After I knock you around a little," Marquard said, closing in once more, "I'm going to pass you around to my boys. Maybe sell you off to all the gangs you've been hounding. I bet there are lots of guys who would love to give you a little payback."

Dusk stayed low, raising her good arm and pushing the barrel of her gun directly against Marquard's knee. She knew she was leaving herself open to another blow from The Thunderfist but she thought it worth the risk. Just as Marquard slammed the glove down atop Dusk's head, she fired her gun, pulling the trigger twice in rapid succession. At such close range, the bullets tore through skin and bone, eradicating Marquard's knee. He howled in agony, his screams lost in the crackling sounds of his glove striking human flesh. Dusk twitched, her eyes opening wide. The scent of burning skin filled the air, its sickly sweet stench repulsing Marquard. He stumbled back, his legs crumbling beneath him. He landed hard, tears of pain stinging his eyes.

Marquard lay there for several moments before he felt hands pulling him upright. Through the haze of agony, he recognized some of the men who crewed the zeppelin. "Get me onboard," he hissed. He was faint from loss of blood and was suddenly fearful that he might die without having touched The Fourth Nail. The men half-carried and half-dragged him towards the ship while Marquard craned his neck to see Dusk. His glove was still sparking and he was sure that he'd killed her with that last punch. At the very least, she had to be comatose.

"Stop," he wheezed. When his men didn't respond, he shoved one of them away and leaned heavily on another. "Where is she?" he demanded.

One of the men looked at him blankly. "Who?"

"Dusk, you damned fool! Where is she?"

The man shrugged. "We were all hiding when you went out to face her. We heard another gunshot and what sounded like thunder. When we looked out, all we saw was you lying on the ground."

Marquard swallowed in disbelief. "Onboard. Quickly."

The crewmen got him up the ramp and he sagged to the floor next to the box. He snatched it up, already knowing that something was wrong. The tingles he'd felt before were absent. He opened the lid and saw nothing inside. The skull and The Fourth Nail were both gone.

"Should we call Doc Severin?" one of the men asked.

"No." Marquard shook his head, tossing the box aside. There was an air of madness about him but none of the men were brave enough to dare disobey him. "Get this ship in the air."

"But you're hurt…"

"You think I don't know that?" Marquard bellowed, using a nearby pipe to pull himself to his feet. He couldn't stand on what was left of his ruined leg but the other held his weight just fine. He spoke in a clipped, weary voice. "It's all over. I've lost. I'm going to burn in Hell. But I'm going to take this city with me."

✵ ✵ ✵

Dusk was breathing heavily, her mind awash in confusing images and sensations. She thought she felt the floor beneath her rattle as if the zeppelin were in motion... but surely she was imagining it. She opened her green eyes, staring into the darkness. She had called upon lessons learned in the Orient after Marquard's attack. An ancient and very wise man had taught her to detach herself from the pain of the body, allowing her to push on when others would not. Using those skills she had managed to stand up despite the incredible pain in her head and the fact that part of her hair and forehead were singed. She had boarded the zeppelin out of instinct more than anything, hoping that the cowards who served Marquard would not find her. In her current condition, she wasn't sure that she could defeat even one or two of them. To her amazement, she'd found the missing skull almost immediately, She'd picked up the box and dumped its contents into one of her gloved hands, quickly stumbling down a hall and collapsing into a storage room.

Dusk looked down at the skull and at The Fourth Nail, which protruded from it. She could feel some sort of energy coming from it but the fact that she'd not touched it with her bare skin had prevented her from fully realizing what it could do. She set it down on the floor and pulled off her glove. She wasn't looking for salvation; she was hoping that it might heal some of the damage she'd sustained.

Dusk picked up the skull again, this time doing it by gripping the nail itself. Immediately, energy coursed through her and she shivered, barely containing a moan that threatened to escape her lips. A flurry of images cascaded through her mind's eye, secret shames and lingering regrets. She saw men and women who had died at her hands but those images were indistinct, for she felt no guilt over their demise. The Fourth Nail instead focused in on the things that did haunt her: Sue sitting alone in a darkened hospital room, sobbing; a funeral held in the pouring rain – a funeral that Dusk attended from the shadows, apart from her family; and finally a house aflame, putting a final closing moment on a life that was forever lost to her.

When the moment had passed, she felt liberated, as if those dark tidings had been wiped away forever. Beneath her mask, her lips moved into an unfamiliar position: a grin. She felt renewed, both spiritually and physically. She set the skull aside and stood up, focusing her acute hearing on the voices she could hear outside. She recognized Marquard, but his voice sounded strained.

"Get us there now!" he was saying. "I want to leave City Hall in ruins!"

Dusk took a moment to check her pistols, ensuring that she had a full clip in each. She knew that Roland would prefer that she take Marquard alive but she had no such qualms. The guilty needed punishing and touching The Fourth Nail had not softened her stance on that. The legal system could not be counted on to handle scum like Marquard. The man was very wealthy, which meant that he could buy and sell men of influence.

After taking a deep breath, Dusk yanked open the door... and came face-to-face with two men brandishing rifles. They smiled at the look of surprise in her face.

"Boss!" one of them yelled. "We found her, just like you said."

Marquard hobbled into the hallway, leaning heavily on the shoulder of a brawny crewman. He grinned like the Cheshire Cat. "Bet you didn't expect this, did you?"

"No," she admitted.

"One of my men spotted your blood. You left a trail down the hall. I told them to set up shop outside the door and wait for you. We could have burst in and killed you but that would have been too quick for you. I want you to see me when I triumph."

"Triumph?" she asked, scorn lacing her words. "You're going to end up dead, one way or another. "If I don't kill you, the loss of blood will. If you had any sense, you'd be taking this ship to the hospital, not City Hall."

Marquard made an ugly face and raised his gloved hand towards her. It crackled with malevolent energy. "You saw up close what my glove can do... this ship can do that a hundred times over. I'm going to carve my initials on the city map. No one will ever forget who I was!"

Dusk's eyes softened a bit. "I pity you. I can only imagine what made you like this, so desperate to prove your worth. It only makes me want to help you somehow."

"I'm going to shove this fist down your throat," Marquard said, grinning. When he showed his teeth, Dusk could see blood seeping from the gaps in his teeth. He was dying and she wasn't entirely sure it was from the gunshot wound she'd given him. The madness that filled his eyes had been present before she'd ruined his knee. Was it possible that he was really and truly sick in some way that went beyond the mental?

Dusk decided it didn't matter in the end. Marquard was a threat to everyone around him and like a rabid dog; he had to be put down. She raised both of her hands quickly, using her pistols to force up the barrels of the two rifles that had been pointed at her face. One of the men discharged his weapon, which was not the smartest of actions while onboard a zeppelin. The bullet ripped through the ceiling and vanished in the upper confines of the vessel.

Dusk moved far quicker than the men in Marquard's employ. Before the gunmen could point their weapons at her again, she had fired both of her pistols straight into their faces. Their bodies hadn't even hit the ground before she'd backhanded the man holding Marquard up. He slammed against the wall and dropped like a sack of potatoes. Without anyone to support him, Marquard did likewise. He landed on his side, The Thunderfist beneath him. It flooded his body with electricity and he began to flop like a fish. If Dusk hadn't kicked him onto his back with the rubber sole of her shoe, he probably would have died.

"Not yet," Dusk whispered coldly. "Not yet."

❀ ❀ ❀

Marquard woke up with the feeling of warmth on his skin. Pain in his shoulders and wrists quickly roused him and he discovered that he was tied with his back to

"*Boss! We found her, just like you said.*"

a tree. Several hundred feet away, his zeppelin was in flames on the ground. Smoke traveled high into the night sky. "The Fourth Nail," he muttered under his breath.

"I left it onboard. I don't know if the flames will destroy it… but I think it's too tempting for men like you." Dusk stepped around the tree, looking towards the inferno. She'd killed almost every member of the zeppelin's crew, leaving alive only two men: both fellows who seemed genuinely unaware of their employer's full plan. Dusk was a cold-blooded killer when necessary but she was human enough to understand that sometimes people made mistakes.

"Why didn't you kill me?" Marquard asked, his voice sounding painfully hoarse. "You gonna turn me into the cops? Didn't think that was your style."

"It's not. But there's something I'd like to do first." Dusk turned to face him and her eyes gleamed like emeralds. "I'm going to show you my face."

Marquard blinked in surprise, wondering what the woman was up to. He didn't particularly want to see her face, not under these circumstances. He knew that she valued her identity and if he knew who she was, then he was doomed. There was no way she'd let him live. Childishly, he closed his eyes tightly, as if that would stop what was coming.

"Look at me," Dusk commanded but Marquard just shook his head. The woman reached out and gripped him by the chin, squeezing until the pain became almost too much to bear. "Look at me," she repeated.

Marquard finally relented, opening his eyes. His gaze fell upon the hidden mysteries beneath Dusk's mask and for the briefest of seconds, he recognized the face he saw there. And then he was lost in the multitude of sins he'd committed, every one of them crashing down upon him. A man who had gone so far to try and avoid facing his crimes now found his soul burdened by them. Every scream he'd caused echoed back at him now and all the pains he'd inflicted, both great and small, now wracked his flesh. He screamed and it was a pitiful thing that echoed long into the night.

Chapter VI.
Family Matters

Sue Timlin was soaking in the tub when her phone rang. It was nearly three in the morning and she ached from head to toe but it never occurred to her to ignore the call. She stepped from the bath, wrapping a towel around her lithe form. She tiptoed across the floor, leaving little puddles in her wake, and raised the receiver to her ear. "Yes?"

Roland sounded quite excited on the other end of the line. In the background, she could hear many voices and a few sirens. "She did it, doll. Dusk got him. Apparently he was planning to use some zeppelin to get out of town or something. The boys from the lab say they've never seen anything like some of this stuff."

Sue smiled wistfully and sat down on the couch. "That's great. Should I tell her thank you?"

"Yeah, do that. No sign around here of The Fourth Nail, though."

"That's probably for the best, don't you think?"

"Yeah," he answered, though there was something in his tone that suggested he didn't really mean it. Sue thought that once someone touched the relic, they probably coveted it a bit too much for their own good. Feeling purified was an addictive thing. "Listen, I'm sorry to have woken you up but I had to tell you. When you get into the office, I'm buying you a big cup of coffee and a Danish."

"Please don't. I'm trying to watch my figure."

"You got nothing to worry about in that regard," Roland said. Sue smiled, knowing that he'd spoken before he'd thought that one through. He wasn't normally so flirtatious.

"How about we celebrate over dinner instead?" she asked. "There's that new restaurant that opened down on Peachtree."

"I'd like that, Sue. We could figure out where we're gonna go with this Dusk thing, huh? Are we going to keep working with her, that sort of thing? I hate the idea of a vigilante but damn, it feels good having Marquard get what was coming to him."

Sue frowned slightly, glad that he couldn't see her face. "That sounds great, Roland. Listen, I better get back to bed. See you in a few hours."

She set the phone back onto its cradle and leaned forward, clasping her hands in front of her knees. She was glad that Roland wasn't gung-ho about catching Dusk anymore but she wasn't sure she wanted him thinking of her as his new best friend, either.

"Penny for your thoughts?"

Sue laughed and shook her head. She didn't bother turning to face the person who'd spoken. "You wouldn't like them."

"Tell me."

"Roland and I are having dinner tomorrow night. He wants to talk about how we can work with Dusk."

"That sounds promising."

Sue's eyes drifted over the pictures on her wall. They lingered on the ones where she was happily smiling and then they moved on to the ones where the mood was much more somber. She remembered the deaths of her mother and father, their bodies burned almost beyond recognition. She remembered their funeral, when she'd stood alone over their casket, tears streaming down her face. She'd sworn to do whatever she could to avenge them. That had led her to working with Roland and the police… and to Dusk.

"He won't like that I've been keeping this from him," she said at last. "Roland is going to feel like I've been playing him for a fool."

"All relationships have secrets. Just look at us."

Sue finally gave in and glanced over at the figure that stood near the couch. It was Dusk, her clothing splattered with blood. "Did you have to kill him?"

"Marquard? Yes. You knew that I would."

"I still don't like it. You show him his sins, let him live out the rest of his life trying to make amends."

"Like I did with Benny the other night? They're vegetables after they see my face. It's actually kinder to put a bullet in their brains."

Sue smiled remorsefully. "You need to get out of those clothes. You smell like smoke."

"Mind if I crash here tonight?"

"You know I don't." Sue stood up. "Let me go draw you a fresh bath and get you some towels."

Dusk touched her arm as she started to go past. "Sue. Thanks for all you do for me. I need you."

Sue gave her a quick hug. "It's okay. What else are sisters for?"

THE END

It's all Ron Fortier's fault
by Barry Reese

I know what you're thinking: you hear that all the time. But this time, it's true. You see, Ron gets a lot of great pulp ideas and there aren't enough hours in the day for him to write them all himself. This leads him to frequently throw down the gauntlet for the Airship 27 gang, challenging us to take a kernel of an idea and run with it.

In this case, Ron wanted to know if any of us could create a female hero in the mold of The Shadow or The Spider - in other words, someone who might be sexy and sensual but not someone for whom those qualities were her stock-in-trade. He wanted someone deadly and maybe a little bit frightening.

I was immediately taken with the notion. You see, I've written a few strong-willed female characters before and I enjoy taking some preconceived notions and turning them on their ear. The character of Dusk appeared almost fully formed in my mind and I whipped off the details, sending them to Ron before the day was through. Thankfully, he was taken with the concept.

Coming up with the character was easier than actually writing the story, however. For some reason, I kept going back and revising this story, until I'd completely scrapped the entire thing and started new no less than three times. There just seemed to be something missing – I liked the main characters and the central mystery surrounding The Fourth Nail was so riveting that I decided to use it again in a future Rook story. So what was wrong?

It felt all too straightforward. I wanted a twist, something that would take what we thought was obvious and twist it around. When I came upon the notion that maybe Sue wasn't actually Dusk, I thought I was on to something. All the hints about what led to her sister becoming Dusk aren't just throwaways, either. I'd like to return to these characters and delve into the full story at some point.

About The Fourth Nail: it's an actual part of Christian myth, though an obscure one. I came across a few details about it while searching for occult conspiracies on the net and was taken with it. One can easily see how it could have become a bigger part of our cultural mythology, joining The Ark of the Covenant or The Shroud of Turin, but for some reason it hasn't caught on. Indiana Jones was confronted with the legend in The Further Adventures of Indiana Jones # 11 & 12, published by Marvel Comics in 1983.

If you're interested in learning more about the often-confusing history of The Fourth Nail legend, I recommend you try 4thnail.com, which was a tremendous help to me. If you'd like to see more Dusk, begin the letter writing campaign to Ron Fortier now. I'll be lurking in the shadows with my MacBook Pro, ready to crank out a few more tales when the call comes.

BARRY REESE- has been writing professionally for nearly a decade, with stops at Marvel Comics, Wild Cat Books, West End Games, Moonstone Books, Airship 27, and ProSe Productions. Though primarily known for THE ROOK CHRONICLES, he has also had the opportunity to work on characters as diverse as The Avenger, The Green Hornet, The Black Bat and Doctor Satan. In addition to his pulp adventure fiction, he is the author of the horror novel RABBIT HEART.

Barry can frequently be found on Facebook and at his official website, http://www.barryreese.net.

AFTERWORD
Meet the Mystery Men

Doesn't that have a really nice, pulp ring to it? The term Mystery Men started floating around the pulp world along about the time masked avengers started popping up both on the radio and in the ten cent magazines. First there was the Shadow, then came the Whisperer and Green Hornet. Soon one couldn't tune in without crossing paths with one vigilante or another. And by the time they invaded the actual pulps, hero pulps exploded across the newsstands of America. The Spider, the Moon Man, the Avenger, Domino Lady, the Black Bat, etc. ad infinitum. It seemed everywhere one turned there was some new character donning a mask, or argus globe or purple scar or—whatever and vowing to fight injustice as a champion of all that was good and decent in the world.

So here we are at Airship 27 Productions having a grand time pumping out terrific new adventures of all these classic pulp personalities and actually overlooking one of the true hallmarks of the genre; that of inventing brand new Mystery Men. Of course that light bulb didn't pop on instantly. Several of our regular writers had been toying with the idea of inventing their own, original pulp heroes and we'd had several discussions on this lively topic. But it wasn't until B.C. Bell sent me his Bagman stories that I began to see true potential here for expanding our line and at the same time staying true to our pulp directive. Hell, I'd even gone down this same road with my own character, Brother Bones. (And before you ask, yes, there will be more Brother Bones coming your way soon. I promise.)

Thus I put out a call to our group of stalwart pulp scribes asking them to give us new pulp heroes; keep them in the 1930s setting, but invent their own characters and while they were at it maybe spin the conventional themes on their rear ends. You see, there were very few female masked avengers in those glory days of the pulps. Honestly, I can only think of one. So this would be a challenge as well. Happily the response was overwhelming and within a few weeks we had enough ideas, suggestions and actual submissions to fill not one, but two volumes of our new MYSTERY MEN (& women).

(Note, there was no way we were going to mouth-mumble a tongue-twister title, thus the little caboose add-on still made it clear the female avenger variety would be present as well.)

I'm damn excited about this first volume. You are about to meet some very cool, fun—and, yes—dangerous figures. Aaron Smith's Red Veil is a very deadly widow from the old school while David Boop's grim battler comes off the football fields into a head-on collision with the mob. Then there's Barry Reese's mysterious Dusk on the hunt for a powerful religious artifact that has to be kept out of the wrong hands at all cost. Of course, the one familiar mask in this book (familiar to loyal Airship 27 readers, that is) is B.C. Bell's terrific Bagman. After his sensational debut in his own TALES OF THE BAGMAN, (still available at Amazon, Barnes & Noble online etc.) it was only fitting that he kick off this new series.

Coming next time you are going meet people like Dock Doyle, Red Badge, Mistress Palladium and the Brown Recluse. Believe me, pulp fans, the fun is just getting started.

As always, thanks for your support and remember, you can find all our titles at our on-line catalog: airship27hangar.com.

'Til next time, stay well and enjoy – AIRSHIP 27 PRODUCTIONS – Pulp Fiction for a New Generation.

Ron Fortier
9/22/2010
Fort Collins, Co.
(airship27@comcast.net)
(www.airship27.com)

AFTERWORD PART TWO

It's hard for me to think that eleven years have come and gone since I first that original Afterword to this amazing series. Lots and lots of water has passed under this title's bridge. Translation, lots of great stories featuring some truly amazing New Pulp writers and their unique, bizarre characters. In the end, we can't help but believe the series has become a success for us and our readers continue to support the concept.

Along the way we made new friends and lost old ones. That's just the way time works. But for those who have left us, their stories continue to live on in these pages. Which was the driving force in our decision to reprint these early volumes of Mystery Men (&Women). As I write this, Volume 8 is in production with number already half filled with submissions. Guess you can say there is no end in sight for all you pulp lovers.

Art Director Rob Davis, yours truly and all the Airship 27 family, our marketing guru Michael Vance, to all our proof-readers, writers and artists want to thank each and every one of you for your continued support. Our promise to you is to continuing delivering the finest in brand new pulp fiction, both in dazzling art and riveting stories.

Ron Fortier
2/9/2022
Fort Collins, CO
(airship27@comcast.net)
(www.airship27.com)

Airship
27

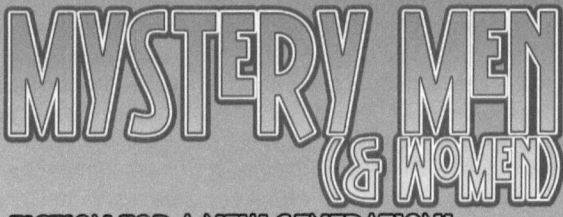